Cesaltina da Cunha is the author of *A Cowgirl and Her Horse* and *Growing Up with Cowgirl Spirit*. Born in Portugal but having lived most of her life in South Africa, she now lives in the UK and works as a self-employed carer throughout England, Wales and Republic of Ireland.

2

For Daddy and Alma, two people rich in simple treasures who showed me that love sees no colour.

For my sister, Paula, who has lived through the challenges of growing up in a mixed culture society, without prejudice.

And for my niece, Amelia, who came into our world on 27 January 2020.

With you all, my story has come full circle.

Cesaltina da Cunha

WINTER'S BREATH

AUSTIN MACAULEY PUBLISHERS™

LONDON · CAMBRIDGE · NEW YORK · SHARJAH

A CIP catalogue record for this title is available from the British Library.

ISBN 9781528999168 (Paperback)
ISBN 9781528999175 (ePub e-book)

www.austinmacauley.com

First Published (2020)
Austin Macauley Publishers Ltd
25 Canada Square
Canary Wharf
London
E14 5LQ

To my sister, Paula, for sharing with me the challenges of growing up in a mixed culture society.

To Rebecca Slack at Austin Macauley for her patience and understanding of my scepticism.

To the team at Austin Macauley who have made this work possible.

Early June 1979

They stepped outside under a moonless sky. Before climbing into the car, she lingered for a moment and just stood there listening to the silence. The town of Uitenhage had yet to wake up as they drove quietly north along Market Street towards the railway station. Amelia and her father drove in silence past the petrol garage and through pale pools of light cast by the streetlamps. A stray dog who stood watch at the end of town, with its head lowered and eyes shining yellow from the car's headlights, was the only witness to their departure. Arriving outside the stone building, Amelia kissed her father on the cheek, and climbed out the car, her breath making clouds in the chill air.

"I'll see you soon, Papa." And with a final wave, she bid her father goodbye, and climbed the three steps to the station's main entrance.

The cold air permeated the clothing draped over her thin body. She wore a thin cardigan over a long-sleeved cotton dress, a woollen hat and scarf and a trench coat which looked too big for her small frame. The station building was empty except for the elderly white man with glasses down on the bridge of his nose, sitting behind the ticket kiosk. Amelia spoke into the glass window misting it up, "One way to Cape Town, please."

He looked up, eyeing her suspiciously at first, then quizzically as if surprised. Her delicate hand retrieved the ticket through the tiny opening in the glass at the bottom of the counter as she smiled back at him, "Thank you."

The old man looked on as she made her way to the far end of the small departure lounge.

With a slim smile pursing his lips he said, "The next one's due in half an hour." He was still staring at her when she bowed her head, acknowledging his announcement. On the wall above the exit to the platform, a giant clock marked away time, the second hand moving precisely with each tick. Occasionally, Amelia caught the old man looking at her and wondered what was going through his mind. He seemed harmless, yet the fact that he was white made her shudder. She knew full well what the white people thought of her race. They were neither black nor white, only something in between. They were a scorned, degraded race, pitied like dogs, and treated with disdain accused of pilfering all moral values. It wasn't easy being coloured. Her father was a white immigrant from Europe who had arrived in the early sixties, penniless, in search of high hopes for a better future. Her mother was coloured, eldest daughter of nine, shunned by her family for marrying a white man. Why could no one see that love has no colour? There was beauty in mixed blessings, that's what Amelia believed, and she lacked nothing that white girls her age had. For one thing, she had a rare gift, a raw talent. She could transform a blank canvas into a masterpiece. She could paint whatever came into her mind and her paintings would come alive with vibrant colours, rich textures and depth. She was talented. She knew that with an innocent arrogance, and she felt no different to anyone else. "Never give up who you are for anyone else," her father would always say. Her mother, on the other hand, had endured the angst and bitterness of apartheid in a country ravaged by racial prejudice and segregation, even by her own people.

Her thoughts were interrupted by a sharp whistle outside.

"There's your train," the old man said nonchalantly.

She nodded, picked up the brown suitcase and walked outside to the platform. The train was still a way off, but she could see the puffs of smoke in the distance as they floated upwards towards the darkened mass of sky. The air was dry and crisp, and it bit into the soft features of her face with an icy vengeance. Amelia stood waiting for the approaching locomotive, her warm breath drawing picture clouds all their own. Her skin tingled from the cold, and she could feel the tip of her delicate nose turn a shade of pink. She sucked in the cool scent of winter and held it deep in her lungs before tugging the coat closer to her. As the train approached, the loud sound was deafening, drowning the old man's call until Amelia felt a tug at her coat.

"You forgot this," he said, handing her the large leather-clad folder she'd forgotten next to the bench.

"Thank you," she said, and flashed him a smile. She boarded the train and waved at the old man as he stood on the platform staring after her. The train was already moving as she walked through to the second-class carriage, catching a glimpse of the old man as he waved his wool cap in the air.

Amelia knew of the art fair that took place in Cape Town. It was a big occasion, a place where the country's finest artists congregated for a week's exhibit of their works. Her father, who had a great appreciation for art, had prompted Amelia to go, and had saved up enough to cover the trip and her entry fee for the exhibition. Although keen to accompany her, it would have meant leaving her mother on her own, and many more hours of overtime at the factory. Amelia brimmed with confidence and reassured him. After all, she was already 19 and not averse to the ways of the world. What would be so difficult? She had everything she needed; registration paper, entry fee, her best work yet, and accommodation at a little motel on the outskirts of the city. She had several pieces that should fetch handsomely, and then she would be able to repay her father, something she felt compelled to do even though she was his only child, and he her greatest fan.

In the carriage compartment, she tried not to stare at the other occupants. Third class, she knew, was normally reserved for blacks, coloureds and Asians, but second class was for 'poor whites'. Sitting across her was a white family, a mother, father and two small boys. Why did the world have to be so cruel? And why were you judged by the colour of your skin? Her father had brought her up to learn that man was not considered better by what he owned, or even where he came from, but rather by the good that he did. Why should the colour of one's skin make such a difference? She felt compassion, but they were indifferent and devoid of emotion. Their displeasure of being in the same proximity as her clearly showed in the way they avoided looking her way or acknowledge her presence, and Amelia chose to divert her thoughts to the passing landscape.

The train was due to back-track inland again before going on to Oudsthoorn and George, after which the line ran parallel to the Indian Ocean, and the train would make several more stops before reaching Cape Town. With the day still ahead, Amelia closed her eyes and tried to sleep, the monotonous chucking sound of the train being the only thing in her head. From time to time, the sharp whistle up front would startle her and she'd open her eyes to find four sombre faces staring at the wood panels behind her. When midday came, the four occupants shyly glanced at the packed lunch in a wicker basket which the mother rested on her lap. Wrapped in faded cheesecloth, a small bread each, cheese and some dried meat. The youngest of the boys smiled and offered her, much to the shocked surprise of his mother, a piece of his bread. Amelia smiled at him and was about to take it when the sharp slap came down over the boy's head. The look on his father's face showed scorn, and the mother took away the boy's parcel, putting it back in the basket. Taken by surprise, the boy lowered his gaze down to the floor and never looked up again. Amelia was overcome by a strange sadness. Reaching up for the suitcase above her head, she took the carefully wrapped lunch her mother had prepared and sat down to eat it. There was a chicken sandwich and a piece of her favourite cheese, an apple, plums, and a beautifully ripe pomegranate from the tree in their garden. In the leather folder Amelia had a painting of the pomegranate tree in full bloom, its branches laden with richly coloured fruit so vivid and alive that you could almost reach out and pick one, or two.

Eating only half of her lunch, Amelia left the compartment and trailed down the long narrow corridor in search of the lavatory. Once inside the tiny cubicle, she wondered how an obese person would fit comfortably enough without feeling trapped and claustrophobic. In the end, she supposed that in second-class bathroom vanities were not a priority that needed consideration. Closing the narrow door behind her, she stood at the half-opened window in the corridor for a long while, admiring the landscape, and gaining inspiration to pour into her work. Heavy clouds flew overhead like timid souls fleeing the wrath of the storm, and Amelia saw a land restless with change. She ventured as far as the dining car and got a glimpse of the interior through the glass paned door. There were tables and chairs padded with thick upholstery, drapes on the windows that provided sensual light into the room, ornate candelabra, and silverware on each table, which even had small glass vases with fresh flowers. What a difference the first class was. In case she would forget, above the door to the restaurant, engraved on a shiny polished brass plate, it clearly said, 'Whites Only/*Slegs vir Blanke*'. How far removed from these people she felt. Catching her reflection in the window, she turned and walked away. She knew she was different. She was not like other coloured people. Her skin was not brown but the colour of amber, as if gently bathed by the sun. Her eyes black like olives, and her hair was a rich deep chocolate colour, with soft luscious curls that cascaded down the top of her back. The only part she suspected might give her away, were the full lips which accentuated her very sensual mouth. Walking back, she felt the train slow down as the sharp whistle blew mercilessly piercing her eardrums. They were approaching a station. As she neared the compartment, her travelling companions existed holding all their belongings between them. The little boy who had offered her his bread looked back at her and smiled a shy smile. She smiled back and stood at the window as she watched him step onto the cement platform. The train stopped just long enough to let them off and left the siding without delay. No one had got on which meant she had the compartment all to herself.

There was comfort in being alone. She released the hard flap that covered the window and sat back resting her head against the high seat, the ripe pomegranate in her hand. They were travelling through the Karoo towards Oudtshoorn, and the vastness of the open spaces reminded her of a giant canvas, bare and waiting for the skilful strokes of her brush. Dusk would come soon, and the dry barren landscape was slowly moulding itself into the darkening sky, the colours melting into dark hues of greys and charcoal. Sitting crossed legged on the wide seat, she sank her teeth into the pomegranate seeds, savouring their succulent sweet flavour and closing her eyes as she allowed the sweetness to tickle her taste buds. For a while, Amelia lapsed quietly into a world of her own, enjoying the sensation while contemplating her chances of success at the fair. The leather flaps on the windows leading to the corridor were pulled down, keeping her space private, shutting out any disturbance, but a soft knock on the glass door made her sit up. She opened the door and came face to face with a tall and distinguished looking man.

"Yes?" Amelia managed, wiping her mouth with the back of her hand, startled by the intrusion.

"Hel–hello. My name is Samuel. Samuel Johnston." Not sure of what to do next, he offered to shake her hand. She remained still, eyeing him suspiciously, saying nothing.

"I'm sorry. I didn't mean to frighten you." he appeared non-threatening, but Amelia was wary.

"I saw you earlier today, at the restaurant car," he said, without moving.

"Yes. I'm sorry. I was just looking –" she was about to give an explanation, when he interrupted her.

"Yes, I know. Why didn't you come in?"

"Because."

"May I ask why?"

"Because I'm not allowed to," she replied indignantly.

"Why ever not?" He looked puzzled.

"The sign says whites only."

He stepped back, taken by surprise.

"And I'm coloured."

A boyish grin erupted into a chuckle, which prompted a girlish giggle, and they both laughed.

"You find that funny," she added.

"Rather," he replied, stretching out his hand.

"You said your name is Samuel? I'm Amelia...Amelia Reis." She smiled and shook his hand.

"Could I sit down?" he asked, gesturing towards the compartment.

"If you like."

"I'm travelling alone, and the company in the restaurant car appeals to me very little." He sat down opposite her and appeared to be well at ease.

"So, where are you travelling to, Amelia?"

She looked him over with a critical eye. He was older, maybe in his late twenties. He was tall, fair hair and with piercing green eyes. His clothes depicted style and good taste. His hands were slender, with long fingers and clean cut nails. She observed him from his head to his black polished leather shoes, all the while looking for a sign of some sort, not sure what she hoped to find.

"I'm going to the art fair in Cape Town." She smiled. He was hanging on to her every word.

"Are you an artist?" He was curious.

"Yes. I do portraits and still life, but mostly landscapes."

"How very interesting." He was amused. Something about her was hypnotic. He felt captivated by her smile and natural beauty, and he wanted to know more, much more about her.

"I have some of my work with me. That's why I'm going there." She got up, unaware he was watching her, and brought the leather-clad folder from the baggage rack above. She opened the folder to display an array of colour he had never seen. As he passed from one painting to another, he was stunned by the degree of depth and detail. He held up a seascape, "Where did you learn to paint like this?" Her talent overwhelmed him.

"I started drawing when I was little. I guess I just got better as I got older," she answered with pride, yet unpretentiously.

"How old are you?" He almost winced as soon as he asked. "Don't answer that. It's none of my business."

"Nineteen," she answered, sitting back against the seat. "Does it matter?"

"No. Of course not. It's just that you have such clarity and depth for one so young. Where do you get your inspiration from?" he asked, intrigued.

"Just about everything, I guess. My father taught me to find beauty in everything I see. I paint what I see, and I feel what I paint."

Samuel straightened, and said, "You know what I see when I look at these paintings?"

"What?"

"I see you. I don't think I've ever seen anyone as clearly as I see you," he murmured. He paused, and then added, "Your father must be very proud." He picked up the seascape again and a wooded landscape in autumn.

"Are they for sale?"

"Of course, all of them are," she replied eagerly, smiling at him.

"How much do you want for these two?" he asked, after admiring them once more.

"Two thousand each," she blurted out without even thinking. That was more money than they were worth, but to her surprise, he accepted.

"Sold! Ms Reis, you have yourself a deal."

She could hardly believe it. Four thousand Rand. That was more money than her mother earned in a month at the plastics factory.

"But I suggest you hold onto your paintings until I've paid you for them. In the meantime, how about we celebrate your first sale?"

"Celebrate?" she asked, confused.

"Allow me to take you to dinner," he said, grinning.

"To dinner?" she asked, puzzled.

"Yes. I'll wait for you in the dining car."

She could feel a surge of panic rise deep in her stomach. The dining car was strictly for whites. What was he asking of her? She would be asked to leave, or worse, thrown out and humiliated.

"Thank you but I can't. I wouldn't feel comfortable. Besides I'm not allowed in there."

Taking her hands in his, he looked straight into her eyes, "Amelia, have dinner with me tonight, please." The look in his eyes made her feel warm, and an oddly strange sensation came over her. She felt drawn to him, enigmatically, and taking a deep breath, agreed. Watching him walk down the narrow corridor, she felt a strange sense of trepidation.

Was it fear or nervousness? She was unsure of whether to be elated or over cautious but decided not to dwell too much on what she was feeling.

From her brown suitcase, she took out a pale blue chiffon dress, long sleeves with a low square neckline and a dark blue satin sash, which was stitched just below the bustline. The sash tied at the back, and accentuated her full breasts adding a little more cleavage. The blue of the simple dress accentuated her lush, dark tresses as they fell in small waves down her back. She looked into the tiny mirror on the opposite wall, and pinched her cheeks, and a soft hue of pink rose to the surface of her delicate skin. She decided to leave the trench coat behind on the seat, shut the compartment door, and made her way towards the front of the long train.

As Amelia entered, the restaurant car became silent, and people turned to stare. In her head, she could hear a hammer pounding above screaming voices, *Whites Only – Whites Only*, and she stopped ready to run. Samuel looked her way in awe, slowly making his way towards her. Suddenly, he could think of nothing to say, nothing that would make sense.

"You look amazingly beautiful." He put her hand over his left forearm and escorted her to their table in a quiet corner. Candlelight cast subtle silhouettes around the room. Soft music played in the background, and the aroma of fine cuisine permeated the air, intoxicating all her senses and making her feel more famished than ever. Samuel was greatly attentive. She smiled as he skilfully poured wine into the long-stemmed glasses.

Aware that all eyes were on her, she innocently asked, "Do you think they suspect?"

Samuel smiled, and nodded his head side-to-side, amused by her innocence.

"No, Amelia. I think they're staring at you because they've never seen anything so beautiful," he answered with unwavering sincerity.

"Are you sure?"

"Absolutely. Now why don't you stop worrying about what others think, and think about what you'd like to eat for dinner instead?" He was doing everything he could to distract her, while at the same time taking in every facet of her. Her face, devoid of any make-up, the luscious pink lips, the tiny pearl drop earrings, and the way a simple dress draped her slender body like an extravagant ball gown. Cupping her left hand with his, he lifted the wine glass in a toast.

"Let's drink to your success! May Cape Town be the start of a bright new future for you Amelia." The clinking of glasses drew attention to their table once again, but Amelia found herself easily becoming relaxed in his presence. Dinner was turning out to be pleasantly enjoyable and fun.

"So, tell me. How long are you planning to be in Cape Town?" he asked.

"I want to sell all my paintings first," she answered, before sipping at her wine. Her sensuous lips touched the rim of the glass, and Samuel had to sit back, his upper body moving away. He had fallen into her eyes, lost in their striking darkness, and suddenly his appetite was gone, and the roast beef he had eyed so hungrily seemed dry and tasteless in his mouth. He was taken by her. The way her lips moved when she spoke, her flawless skin, and the exotic almond shaped eyes. He could feel them peering into his soul. Filled with a strange sense of curiosity, he wanted to know everything about her. Looking deep into her hypnotic eyes, he sensed a magical and mysterious place where an ancient womanly wisdom probably dwelled, despite her tender age. There was a certain pride about her, an air of dignity; he had noticed it earlier, a kind of gravity tempered with grace. Amelia smiled at him, lost in a reverie of fine taste as she savoured every morsel of the three-course meal.

"That was very delicious, thank you," she expressed with a wide smile, as she leaned forward, placing both elbows on the table, totally disarming Samuel.

"I'm glad you enjoyed it," he managed, finding it difficult to speak.

"Would you care for some tea or coffee perhaps?"

"Tea would be really nice."

The dining car was slowly becoming empty as guests retired to their compartments, and staff busied themselves cleaning up for the next day's breakfast. Samuel could have watched her all night, taking in every gesture and move she made, her soft smile, and the way her eyes twinkled when she spoke about her art. It was getting late, and they were the last to leave.

Samuel led the way out the dining car, holding the door open for her. Out in the brightly lit corridor, everything was still except for the continuous clanking of the train chugging along on the rail track. The stars sparkled brightly in the blackest of skies, and the night was a marvel of beauty to behold. The air was frigid and biting with an icy coldness against the long windows. Amelia touched the window, but removed her hand quickly, feeling the cold as it shuddered through her body. Samuel put his coat over her shoulders and held the lapels together, as if to keep the warmth in. She could feel the night around her, somehow alive and magical, as if the moonlight laid down a path of silver and the white ice of the stars glittered like hope in the velvet sky. Still standing in front of her, Samuel bent his head towards her face and gently planted a soft kiss on her lips. Startled at first, she withdrew, and pressed her fingers where his lips had touched hers so tenderly.

She looked up at him shyly, as an inexplicable tingling coursed through her whole body. Samuel wondered if she had ever been kissed before, and as if she could read his mind, "No one's ever done that before," she confessed, with such innocence that it overwhelmed him. He wanted to take her in his arms and hold her tight, never letting go. He wanted to feel the touch of her lithe body against his and explore all the womanly curves he imagined beneath her thin dress. Putting a little distance between them, he cupped her face in his hands and kissed her again, this time more passionately. She surprised him by responding.

"Do you find me attractive...Samuel?" she asked, biting her lower lip.

"Yes...Amelia. But it's more than that," he answered, as his hands held her face close to his.

"What does that mean?" she asked, staring into his eyes.

"Frankly, I find it hard to explain."

"Do you want to make love to me?" she asked.

Surprised by her candour, he stepped away, and looked into her eyes, before answering, "Yes Amelia, I want to make love to you...and over again."

Just then the door she was leaning against suddenly gave way, with Amelia falling atop the marble washbasin vanity of the first-class restroom. Samuel quietly closed and locked the door. Amelia looked up at him. He searched her eyes for the longest time, and wordless communication flowed between them. Samuel knelt before her and slipped his hands under her dress. His hands trailed up her long thighs, sending shivers down her back. While it was true that she'd never been with a man before, she was not totally oblivious to desire. For one, she was after all a grown woman of nineteen who was not averse to exploring her own body. And, there had been several occasions where she had witnessed her friends entwined and in passionate embraces. Her best friend had been sleeping with her partner for some time, and she was always eager to share her intimate escapades with Amelia, often leaving very little to imagination. Right now, she felt a deep and burning desire to experience what Sonya often spoke about. Amelia recalled occasions when she had touched herself and how she was overcome with a warm sensuous pleasure. Samuel's hands rested on her hips, under her dress, and when his lips found hers again, Amelia kissed him with abandon. There was more urgency in his touch, more fire within her. She could no longer contain the feeling of desire that surged through her. Samuel's gentle hands moved up to her breasts, over her dress, and Amelia felt herself getting weak at the knees. He seduced her with his warm breath on her ears. By the way his lips gently touched the sides of her neck, and his hands cupped the full breasts. When he kissed her again, the wetness of his mouth made her tingle all over. She nibbled on his lower lip, as he slid his coat off her. It was cold in the restroom, but Amelia felt only a fire welling deep in her being. She wondered if Sonya had ever felt it this way. Whether her friend's boyfriend had been as gentle as Samuel was being with her. He reached for the satin bow at her back, and gently pulled it apart, then his fingers found the zip, and he pulled the thin dress down carefully, a little at a time. Samuel could not take his eyes off her. Tiny beads of perspiration around her hairline curled the short strands of hair into ringlets, which fell sensuously on her face. Samuel let the dress slip to the floor, and Amelia stood before him, the thin petticoat clinging to her moist body, revealing perfectly sculpted proportions beneath.

Amelia watched as he removed his tie and undid his shirt collar. She moved closer to him, helping undo the buttons, and easing the shirt off his back. His shoulders were broad and narrowed down to a flat stomach and thin waist. She'd often seen men without their tops when they worked outdoors in the middle of summer, but Samuel looked different. His skin was pale, and though she saw no sign of him ever being in the sun, he was in good shape with well-defined muscles. She smiled at him, and playfully tugged at the curly hairs on his bare chest. Samuel lifted the petticoat over her head, and kneeling on one knee, slipped her underwear off, leaving it on the floor. Getting up, he unbuckled his belt, and dropped his pants and briefs to the floor beside hers. They stood facing each other naked, both oblivious to the freezing cold outside. His finger followed the outline of her face, before it rested under her chin. She looked up at him, a searching look in her eyes.

"Tell me to stop and I will…I will," he said, huskily.

But, she didn't. Samuel took her in his arms. His eyes filled with passion and, moving away from the marble vanity, he lifted her against the panelled wall, as she wrapped her legs around his middle. He kissed her. The kiss had so much tenderness and desire, longing to be expressed that neither of them could breathe. The world withdrew from around them, and the sound of the moving train receded into the distance.

Amelia bit her lower lip, and clung to him as he took her, no longer able to hold back. Her short fingernails dug into his back. She uttered a stifled cry as he penetrated her. It hurt, and it felt like a dozen knives were cutting through her insides. She felt pain, and then a warm gush as her innocence flowed out of her, mingled with the wetness of desire. Samuel tried to control his own pleasure but couldn't. He wanted her, all of her. Amelia's whole body pulsated with wondrous sensations, and she clung to him when he tried to pull away. He lowered her legs slowly, and held her in a tight embrace, shielding her from the cold, when he felt her tremble against him. Stepping away from her, he noticed the blood between her legs.

"Does it hurt badly?" he asked, kneeling.

"A little. Not too bad," she lied. It hurt a lot more than she was willing to admit. Sonya had lied to her too, saying that it was only a little uncomfortable.

Her naked body shook slightly, and Samuel draped his coat over her. When he looked into her face, she appeared fragile and vulnerable, and Samuel was overcome with emotion.

He took a handkerchief from his coat pocket, and soaked it with warm water, before gently cleaning between her legs taking care not to hurt her.

"I'm sorry...I shou–" he started to apologise, but she stopped him, running her trembling fingers through his hair.

"Don't be...I could have stopped it too..." she assured him.

He helped her dress before dressing himself. The tiny room had suddenly become cold. Walking out into the corridor, Samuel escorted her to her compartment at the far end of the train. It was dark and cold in there, and somehow it felt strange, different to the way she had left it earlier in the evening. Samuel stepped inside and held her close.

"Stay with me," she whispered, suddenly feeling tired.

Samuel sat beside her, as she put her feet up on the seat. She lay lengthways on the cold seat, her head resting on his lap. He draped her trench coat over her. Amelia closed her eyes and tried not to think of the burning sensation between her thighs. Samuel touched her tousled hair and looked up at the empty baggage rails overhead.

What had he done? He closed his eyes, remembering every minute detail of her body, her scent, and the feel of her as he entered her, taking away what was not his to take. He was aware of a sensitivity toward her that he had never felt toward any other woman, a kind of tender curiosity. Samuel did not return to his compartment. He stayed with Amelia, as she lay on his lap and, drifted in and out of sleep waiting for the dawn of a new day.

For another full day and night, the rumble and tremor continued, as the train approached other stations along its route, an astonishing engineering achievement. The landscape stretched over farmland and veld, through spectacular country, over mountains and across deep valleys, and there were sudden bursts of colour all around in wild, unexpected places. In the privacy of his compartment, Amelia surrendered herself to Samuel's pampering and pleasure. The attraction between them was intense, immediate, overwhelming. Surrendering to him meant abandoning herself completely – and giving up all control. Their intimate moments were tender, commanding, and erotic. Pleasures Amelia could never have imagined in her young mind. There was something primal in the way he read her, following her movements, her gestures and words. The pleasure they gave each other was the greatest either of them had ever known, given with such full hearts, and yet, achieved so simply and naturally. Samuel knew he was not in the hands of a great lover, but in the hands of a woman who was capable of great love.

Amelia stared out the window, fascinated by the sights as the train slowed into Cape Town station. The sky had turned bleak and grey again, and a fine drizzle fell on the high rooftops. The station was a buzz of activity, with people coming and going, whistles blowing, luggage trolleys scurrying around pushed by porters. There were people getting on and some getting off. Amelia stood in the middle of the platform and marvelled at the diverse goings on of the central main station. She took in the sights and sounds and closed her eyes, as if to put away in her mind, the memory of the day. One day, she would paint it on a canvas, and she would remember it just as she felt it then. She opened her eyes, took a deep breath, and walked towards the main doors leading into the building. Her heart sank at the brass sign above the glass-panelled door, 'Whites Only/*Slegs vir Blanke*'. Remembering what Samuel had told her, she turned the solid, heavy brass knob and entered. She could feel her heart pounding in her chest as she waited to be singled out, and when nothing happened, she walked off, her head held high. Samuel found her on the outside of the station building, her brown suitcase and leather folder at her side. The taxi driver deposited her luggage in the boot, whilst Samuel opened the back door of the cab to let her in and climbed in next to her.

"The Mount Nelson," he told the driver. They drove out of the station into heavy traffic and travelled along the outskirts of the city. Amelia looked out the window smiling. Cape Town was deliciously old fashioned, with wide tree lined streets, parks and gardens. The soft drizzle had started to subside, but the air felt colder. Amelia tightened the scarf around her neck and put her cold hands in her coat pockets.

Samuel sat next to her, saying nothing, yet his eyes spoke of a thousand things. Half an hour later, the cab came to a stop outside the entrance of a pink building. Samuel got out first and moved around to open the door for Amelia. She stepped out as if almost afraid to let her feet touch the ground, and let Samuel guide her to the entrance through the revolving doors. In the foyer of the hotel, Amelia looked around in awe. Chandeliers hung from the high ceilings, marble and shiny brass blended into the rich textures of heavy drapes and ornate Persian carpets and rugs. Taking her by the arm, Samuel approached the concierge and booked them in. The porter retrieved their luggage and led the way to the elevator. Inside, Samuel stood close to her taking her hand in his, a smile pursing his lips. The elevator stopped on the second floor and the porter waited for them to pass, before getting out and leading them to room 236. Amelia stared at the brass plate on the door and smiled girlishly at Samuel.

"That's funny," she said, turning to him.

"What is?" he asked, unsure of what she meant.

"The number on the door is 236," she answered, as the porter turned the key and opened the door.

"What a coincidence," she said, stepping into the room.

The porter laid down their luggage on the wooden rack and left, closing the door quietly behind him. Removing her hat and scarf, Amelia wandered around the luxury suite taking in every detail. The large oak four-poster bed was draped with fine chintz fabric with big pillows and cushions. A small coffee table in one corner with matching upholstered armchairs that were covered with a rich burgundy and gold fabric. Fresh flowers on a small dresser, elegant lampshades, a valet stand and the morning paper, all neatly placed. Amelia took off her shoes and let her cold feet warm against the thick carpet fibres. Samuel took off her coat, and then his, and draped them over the back of one of the armchairs. He turned to her, taking both her hands in his and bringing her closer to him, "So tell me why the number 236 is such a coincidence?" he asked, boyishly.

"Well…I was born on the 23th of June," she answered.

"Then I shall consider it my lucky number," he replied.

"Will you be taking me to the motel?" she asked, a little more seriously.

"Of course, if you want me to," he answered.

"Do you want me to go?"

"No." He held her closer, lifting her chin to look him in the eye. "I want you to stay."

"I'll need to get to the exhibition. It starts tomorrow," she said, remembering the reason she had come to Cape Town.

"I have some meetings to attend to, and after that I'm free. I was planning to go back in the next day or two, but I can wait," he offered. "I can drop you off at the exhibition and meet you after my meetings. And you can tell me all about your day."

They would have time to wine and dine, and the evenings showed promise of endless pleasure and unbridled passion. Amelia felt giddy with excitement, even though the niggling thoughts of where it would lead to still dwindled in her mind. She sat on the oversized bed, running her hands along the luxury of the chintz cover, and feeling the padded softness beneath her. She looked around, as Samuel unpacked his things, hanging up his suits, and placing the neatly folded shirts on the wardrobe shelf.

"Would you like to unpack? There's plenty of room here," he said, holding the wardrobe door open.

"Don't have much to put away," she answered, picking up the brown suitcase from where the porter had left it. She placed the suitcase on the bed, and unpacked. Two dresses, a long tweed skirt and polo neck jersey, undergarments and night dress, a thick woollen jersey, some socks and a hessian bag with a hairbrush, toothbrush, a tube of toothpaste, a flannel and a bar of glycerine soap. He watched with tender curiosity, as she laid her belongings on the bed. Life for her seemed so uncomplicated, and of such a simplistic existence, that he almost envied her.

"How about we go shopping tomorrow, after all is done?" he asked.

"Shopping?" she asked.

"Well, you've obviously not brought enough clothes for the trip. So, I think we need to fix that. I know some really great places." There was a boyish excitement about him, as if going shopping was something new he wanted to experience.

She found herself getting just as excited. Not only about shopping for new clothes, but also about being with him. Her father had worked many late hours to save up enough to get her to Cape Town. Now, she was in a fancy hotel room with a man she didn't know, who made her wild with desire, and whom she had given herself freely to. She had crossed the threshold from young adult to womanhood. She was no longer a girl, and she felt a deep change in herself. She was different. She felt it, and she was certain her father would see it too. Amelia put her thoughts of guilt aside and decided instead to enjoy the moment. Samuel was kind and gentle. He wasn't prejudiced, she admired that in him. Sooner or later life was bound to bring someone her way and the same thing might have happened, except that there wasn't anyone she fancied. She looked at him, and with unswerving curiosity decided to take the next few days getting to know him. She would tread slowly, choosing not to ask too much at a time.

She lay back against the stacked pillows and cushions and popped her first question.

"So, how old are you?" It seemed the perfect place to start.

"Twenty-seven," he answered, taken by surprise.

"You look more like thirty," she grinned.

"Does it matter to you?" he asked, unsure.

"Not really. My father is almost seventeen years older than my mother. Age is just a number anyway," she answered nonchalantly. She watched him, as he moved across the room. It was enough for now. There would be time to find out more.

"What about the motel?" she asked, changing the subject.

"I can call, and let them know you won't be coming," he replied.

"Won't they complain?" What if they called her father?

"I'll pay them the full board, and tell them you're staying with a friend instead," he offered.

"Are you okay with that?"

"It's a small price to pay to be with you, but only if you want to of course."

Amelia laced her arms around his neck. Her smile lit up the room. How handsome he looked, and how much she liked being in his arms. Her freshness and innocence fuelled his desire. His admiration for her, already great, increased tenfold. And Samuel knew right then, he would never have enough of her.

The town square was a hive of activity. There were artists from all over the country, and some from abroad as well. All around, stalls were being set up, and rows of easels showed a variety of art, from contemporary to romantic, impressionist to the abstract. Amelia found herself surrounded by replicas of the Monet, Renoir and Cezanne. There were artists whose work could have passed for Guaghin originals, and an artist who duplicated Frida Kahlo's style so closely that it brought a smile to her face. She felt a surge of excitement race through her, as she made her way to the registration table. Many of the entrants appeared to be of an age when people wound down into the obscurity of retirement, yet she understood their passion and dreams of being artists. Her passion for painting had come about by happenstance. At the age of four, her father had bought a box of coloured chalk and a slate board for her to draw on. Finding the board surface too small an area to express herself creatively, she started drawing on the walls of her bedroom, making sure that her creations were hidden from view, and would not be washed off. It was only when she started running out of wall space, that she had the confidence to confront her parents and show them what she'd been up to. Even though she had been a little girl, she remembered the surprised look on their faces well, as she brought her masterpieces into full view. It was also then her father realised that Amelia had a gift. In time, the chalk was replaced by water colours and then by oils. That had been a few years ago. Today, she found herself amongst some of the country's finest artists, but her talent was unequalled for one so young. After collecting her registration, Amelia was directed towards the stall she would be sharing with another artist. Amelia had only one easel which she'd left at home, and she needed to find a way to exhibit her pieces. Samuel, who had been watching from a distance, came to her rescue and paid for two display stands which would accommodate at least four of her larger paintings. He left, but not before reminding Amelia that they had an engagement after the day was done. Amelia kissed him on the cheek, and started to set up, oblivious to the startled admiration of her neighbour and people who stopped to stare. The woman she shared the stall with was of a mature age. Amelia guessed at least in her sixties. She was a quiet, demure woman of medium stature with short grey hair and deep blue eyes. She introduced herself as Emma Harris. As the day passed, Emma confessed to Amelia that she was a reborn artist. Amelia warmed up to her instantly. Emma's easy and gentle demeanour was comforting to Amelia. There was a profound side to her personality which Amelia picked up on, mainly from the swift strokes of Emma's brushes.

"Art has always been my passion," she told Amelia. "And I never gave up on it. But I was never confident enough to paint myself."

"Why not?" Amelia questioned.

"I never believed people would buy my work," she offered, with a reticent smile.

"But your work is so refreshing," Amelia commended, looking at the old woman's love of impressionism depicted in an interpretation of a stream.

"I suppose it's one of the advantages of growing old, you become more confident," she replied heartily.

Amelia was about to put aside the two paintings Samuel had already paid for, when Emma caught sight of them.

"Now that is poetry in motion my dear," Emma admired. "That surf spray comes alive against the rocks," she said, stepping back to admire the seascape some more.

"You can almost hear the fallen leaves rustling in the gentle breeze," she commented about the wooded landscape painting. "Where did you learn to paint like this?" Emma was fascinated and astounded by Amelia's talent.

"You have a gift child, you do," she said, folding her arms and stepping back, taking in the pure colour which made Amelia's paintings come alive.

"You'll sell these for sure."

"They're already sold," Amelia said, confidently.

"Already?" asked Emma.

"Yes, to Samuel, my friend. He was with me this morning." She smiled.

"Well, I'm very thrilled for you. They are beautiful. And so are all the others," Emma said, with sincerity.

Amelia felt a tingle of excitement. Maybe her paintings would sell soon, and that would leave her with more time to get to know Samuel. She found herself thinking of him, and that excited her too.

The weeklong festival continued in a flurry of activity, and by the last day, Amelia had just one painting left to sell. It was a still life of wildflowers which danced with light and colour. The stall she and Emma shared was the centre of much attraction. Amelia sold her last painting and was commissioned to do more for the client who had bought three of her pieces. She put away her earnings, spent the day chatting to Emma, who thrilled her with stories of her days at Fine Arts School, and waited for Samuel to meet up with her later in the afternoon, as had become custom.

By then, Amelia also knew more about her handsome companion. Samuel was an only son. The Johnston Stud was one of the oldest registered with the Dohne Merino Breed Society since Samuel's father established it in the late 1940's. The stud earned international recognition for producing outstanding lamb crops and superior wool quality and was almost completely under Samuel's management. His mother had been a music teacher who gave piano and violin lessons. Sadly, after his mother's death from liver cancer, his father became a recluse, preferring to live alone and he left the stud and the family affairs to Samuel, his only heir. Samuel travelled countrywide, ensuring the sale of new stock and keeping the family heritage secure. His father, who had nursed his mother throughout her debilitating illness, had lost his will for the life he once had. At twenty-seven, Samuel was a wealthy man with a prospering business and an astute financial mind – but he was also a lonely man. From the age of seventeen, he had become involved in the family business, and that had left very little time for anything else. With the loss of his mother, Samuel was forced to take on added responsibilities when his father's interest began to wane. David Johnston had been married to his wife for forty years, and without her he was half a person. Samuel understood that. He also understood that his father had lost his will to live, and that saddened him beyond measure.

The morning before Amelia was due to return home, Samuel had come out of a deep dreamless sleep, and felt as fresh and happy as he did hungry. All his deals had been sealed, future projections for the stud looked handsome, and he was free to spend the last day with Amelia, away from distractions and interruptions.

"How would you like to go sightseeing tomorrow?" he asked, turning to Amelia, as she looked out from the balcony of the second floor, still dressed in the bathrobe which covered her naked body.

"Sure," she replied, coming into the room.

There was a melancholy look about her. She wasn't smiling as she always did.

"You're sad," Samuel observed.

"Yes. I'm leaving tomorrow, and I don't know if I'll ever see you again," she replied, dropping her chin.

"What do you mean? You'll give me your address, and I'll come see you," he said, trying to reassure her.

For the first time since their meeting on the train, Amelia began to understand the divide that Samuel had tried so hard to make her forget.

"Samuel, don't you see?" she said, looking up at him. "It wouldn't work for us. We come from very different worlds." She felt herself getting angry for the first time.

"What are you talking about? And why should that make a difference? Why Amelia?" he asked, trying to understand her change of heart.

"Because I have seen what it's done to my parents. I've seen how my father gets condemned for loving a coloured woman. I've seen how my mother has been shunned for marrying a white man. It's hard for my mother to live amongst her own people with my father, and my father is seen as nothing more than a kaffir lover," she blurted the words, through the tears that had welled up, and when Samuel tried to comfort her she moved away. She didn't want his pity.

"You're wrong to believe that the colour of your skin would make a difference to how I feel about you."

"What can I say or do to convince you?" he asked, panic in his voice.

"I don't think we should see each other again. I don't want to mess up your chances of finding happiness with someone your own kind," she said.

"How can you even think that? You know that's not how I feel Amelia." He was desperate to make her see what was in his heart. "Maybe it's not what we want but it's the best for both of us."

"Amelia, I love you. And I have never been surer of anything in my life. You feel it too, I know you do. Please don't do this," he pleaded.

"Promise me you won't come looking for me," Samuel remained silent. It was not a promise he wanted to keep. "Promise me," she insisted, her voice rising slightly.

"If that's what you want. But you're wrong."

"I'm sorry Samuel." She could not bear to look at him. She could see the waves of confusion, of disbelief, passing across his face. Whatever situation they would face could not be more than the pain she was in. A pain so deep it was a perfect darkness, like a night without moon or stars or end. Every part of her was crying out for him. She wanted to run into his arms and tell him that it wouldn't matter. Her parents had made it through, and they were happy. She wanted to quieten the fear that overcame her at that very moment. It was the fear of never seeing him again, and never again feeling the way she did when she was with him.

"I'm sorry too Amelia. Can I at least see you off at the station tomorrow?" he asked, resignation in his voice.

She nodded but turned away. For a brief moment, Amelia felt that she was making a grave mistake. Samuel was a good man. He had treated her right. He wasn't like the others, cruel and prejudiced. Since boarding the train, they had spent seven days together, and in that time, he had been loving and kind, and ever gentle. Why did she doubt him? How could she not have faith in him when he had so much in her? Maybe that's what true love was, a leap of faith. Like swimming out into the ocean and trusting the waves to bring you back to shore. But she knew it had very little to do with him, and everything to do with a society that was plagued by prejudice and injustices. She lived through that every day of her life, and she didn't want that to destroy what she and Samuel had found in each other.

It was late afternoon when Samuel escorted her to the main station. She was leaving with an extra suitcase filled with the things he had bought for her. She would have those to remind her of their time together. The leather-clad folder was now empty, and as they stood on the platform waiting for Amelia to board, she held a first-class ticket in her gloved hand, "Thank you," she said, raising the ticket. A wry smile crossed his face as he nodded.

"Thank you for everything," she said, fighting hard to hold back the tears.

"You'll be famous someday," Samuel said, with a boyish grin.

"Maybe, some day." She pulled the crimson wool hat down on her head and offered Samuel a handshake. "Goodbye, Samuel."

She hated the weakness that shivered like water through her limbs. Hopelessness lashed through her like the tip of a whip against the inside of her ribcage. To kiss him now would have rendered her powerless. She couldn't afford to end it that way. They had promised each other. Samuel took her hand in his and held it for a while. He wanted to sweep her into his arms and kiss her. He wanted to tell her that he loved her, that his life would be empty without her. But he had to let her go. How could it be that every time he looked at this woman, he loved her more? Thought her more beautiful, more sensual, more amazing? He gently let go of her hand and watched as she turned away to board the train. When she stepped onto the train that morning, without looking back, she took the sun out of the day, and the light right out of his heart.

Through the night, Amelia thought of much. Memories of their nights together rippled through her. She thought of the passionate taste of Samuel's kisses, the possessive gentleness of his caresses, the pleasure and intimacy of being one. She'd never known that kind of pleasure existed or that it could get better each time, as her love for him did. Every part of her being was filled with questionable doubt. Regret for not giving Samuel a chance, and fear of what her father's reaction might be if he found out about them. She knew she had betrayed her father's trust. She had given herself to Samuel with reckless abandon. Discarded were the values and morals of her upbringing. Too tired to think, she drifted off to sleep. She would confide in her parents when the time was right. It was something she would think about later.

The train chugged with effort up the mountain pass before the downwind eased its motion. It was bitterly cold, yet the sky was a bright blue velvet, cloudless and unmoving. Amelia had chosen not to venture into the restaurant car for dinner earlier on, preferring to eat a sandwich in the security of her compartment grateful for the opportunity to be alone. The return trip was uneventful, and Amelia slept most of the way. The train was due to arrive on time, and as the minutes ticked past, so her anxiety grew. What would she say to her parents? Would her mother notice anything different about her? Would her father suspect anything at all? Amelia wondered whether she would have the courage to tell them the truth. What they didn't know couldn't hurt them, she thought, yet she was certain the guilt she felt would betray her. There was no need for her to tell them anything about Samuel, she thought defiantly. He didn't know where to find her. Their time together would be her secret. That way there would be no need to lie. She decided to spare her parents the details of her intimate encounters with Samuel Johnston. It was the sensible thing to do.

The train arrived on schedule, and even though Amelia was filled with strong apprehension, she was relieved to see her father's familiar grin. She would normally have run into his arms, but instead walked slowly towards him, putting her arms around his neck.

"Hallo, Papa." She held him tightly.

"Ola, Princess." He embraced his child with gentle tenderness. She had only been gone a few days, but he had missed her, more than she would ever know.

"So how was the trip? And the show?" he asked, taking hold of the two suitcases she was carrying.

Amelia knew she had to be strong. She had to be careful not to give rise to any suspicion.

"I sold all my paintings and made a serious amount of money," she said, avoiding his glances.

"And this suitcase?" he asked, of the suitcase Samuel had bought for her.

"I did some shopping and brought home a few spoils." She needed to think fast and stay alert.

"Your mother has been worried about you. She hasn't slept all week," her father said, as they walked to the parked car. "You know Ma, she worries for nothing most of the time."

For the first time in her life, Amelia felt uneasy in her father's presence. It had nothing to do with him and all to do with her. She was no longer his little girl. She had crossed the threshold from girl to womanhood, the moment she had succumbed to Samuel's sensual touch. It was an experience she had not been prepared for, yet, it was an experience to which she had totally and completely surrendered herself to.

"So, did you get to meet anyone famous?" her father asked, as he got behind the wheel.

"Not really," she answered, looking out the window.

"Amelia are you okay?" he asked, concern in his voice.

"Of course, why do you ask, Papa?"

"You seem a little distant, that's all."

She turned to look at her father and, tried to smile. Yes, he was right. She was distant. She was afraid. And her mind was filled with thoughts of Samuel.

"I think I'm just tired from the trip. But I'm glad to be home, and I can't wait to tell you and Ma how much my paintings sold for." She tried hard to put Samuel out of her mind, but the memory of him haunted her. How he had made love to her, the tenderness of his embrace. The way he would run his fingers through her tousled hair, and how when his lips touched hers, she would wish for time to stand still. She could think of nothing else. The thought of never seeing him again brought a cold shiver. Had she made the right choice? Could she forget him?

"Well, that is good, no? I am happy that you're home too," her father answered, gently taking her hand in his.

"It's good to be home Papa." She squeezed her father's hand. That part was true. She did miss home, but she missed Samuel a whole lot more.

Amelia kept herself busy finishing the orders she'd been commissioned to do. During the nights, she stayed awake to paint, and she watched new things appear on her easel – landscapes of lonely houses perched among fierce hills and people in shadowlike forms. Her restlessness was not easily appeased, and she could no longer distinguish one moment of her life from another. Events of each day were forgotten as soon as they had passed. During the day, she would set up the easel outside and sit on the bench with the wind scattering dead leaves at her feet. There she could believe life held hope and promise. She tried hard not to think of Samuel, but every so often his face would creep into her mind and, she would try hard to dispel any thoughts of him. Her friends complained that she had become a hermit since her return, but Amelia really wanted to be alone. She was uncomfortable around her parents. Not being able to tell them the truth left her emotionally strained and riddled with guilt. She often imagined Samuel looking at her and thought she heard him call out her name. When Sonya coaxed her into spending the night out with her, it seemed like a good excuse to shut all those thoughts from her mind. But perhaps the night out hadn't been such a good idea. Maybe something she'd eaten or maybe too much alcohol, something she wasn't used to. She felt sick to her stomach as another wave of nausea sent her rushing into the bathroom just in time, her body hunched over the toilet bowl. The vomiting went on for a while until Amelia felt that her stomach was truly empty. She felt light headed and emaciated.

She sat on the edge of the single bed, everything around her was spinning. The churning feeling in the pit of her stomach grew stronger. She'd been out with her friend Sonya the night before. The two of them and a few others had enjoyed a night out dancing and perhaps maybe a little too much drinking.

It was already past seven, and both her parents had left for work. She was alone. She brushed her teeth and rinsed her mouth a few times, hoping to be rid of the sour taste. Her mother would only be back by six, and her father, probably not until much later. She stepped out onto the veranda and took a few deep breaths. The air was crisp, and as it passed through her nose into her lungs, she could still feel the cold bite of winter. The sky was crystal clear, a massive expanse of light sapphire blue. From where she stood, Amelia could see the chimney of the old shed at the far end of their property. Years ago, before her father bought the property, the shed had been used as a workshop by the previous owner. Her father had bought the small holding six years before, but little had been done to revamp the place. She went back inside the house, pulled a thick sweater over her head, and tried to think about breakfast.

Until that moment, Amelia hadn't thought much about what to do with her share of the earnings. She had spoiled her mother with a dress she'd seen on the window at the OK Bazaar and bought some sweet-smelling tobacco for her father's pipe. The rest she kept under her mattress. Her father always said that it was safer and cheaper there than it was in the bank. Standing out on the veranda, earlier on, she'd had an idea. She would need to discuss it with her parents of course, but to her it was a brilliant idea. She would talk to them over dinner.

"I've been thinking about something," she blurted out, whilst the three of them sat down to dinner that evening.

"I want to use some of the money I have left to restore the old shed," she ventured, waiting for the reaction.

"Whatever for?" Her mother was the first to speak.

"Well, I thought that since I'm getting busier with all the commissioned work it would be nice to have more room," she offered, smiling enthusiastically.

"That place is so derelict. It needs a lot of work," her mother said.

"I know, Ma, but we could fix it and then I could have my own studio, and not be as crammed as I am right now," she insisted.

"This is good, no?" her father asked.

"Of course, it is, and it would be like a real artist's studio." Amelia beamed.

"I suppose we could all get stuck in and fix it up," her mother agreed.

"So, it's settled then?" Amelia asked.

Her parents nodded in agreement. Her excitement was infectious.

"We'll go take a look, and see what we can do," her father answered.

"If you're going to get stuck in there, you'll need to build your strength," her mother said, pointing to the food still on Amelia's plate. "You haven't eaten a thing."

"I'm not really hungry, Ma."

She was hungry, but the thought of food made her stomach churn.

For now, she was content with the idea of having her own studio. A place she could call her own. A solitary place to be alone with her thoughts and the nagging concern that she was experiencing bodily changes she didn't quite understand.

The next two mornings were much the same as the ones before. Amelia was beginning to doubt that her nausea was due to anything she'd eaten. Added to that, was something even more uncomfortable than having to lean her head into the toilet bowl. Her private parts had developed an irritation that caused her to scratch herself so hard and long that she would tear the sensitive skin, leaving it raw, inflamed and bleeding. Along with that, was a foul-smelling wet residue that seeped through to her underwear. She feared having caught some incurable disease, and too afraid to confide in her mother, she turned to her friend Sonya for advice. Unsure herself, Sonya discussed Amelia's problem with her aunt, a nursing sister at the town's provincial hospital. Together, Amelia and Sonya paid Margret a visit, hoping she would be able to explain.

"When did you start to feel the itching?" Margret asked Amelia, as they sat on a low wall surrounding the hospital parking lot.

"A week ago, but it feels like it's getting worse," Amelia answered shyly. It wasn't easy talking to someone else about something so private and personal.

"Do you feel anything else?" asked Margret.

Amelia nodded, then said, "Just really sick in the morning."

Margret looked closely at Amelia, and then at Sonya.

"Amelia, I need to ask you a very personal question," her voice had lowered, and Amelia felt fear well up in the pit of her stomach.

"Have you been with anyone Amelia?"

"What do you mean?" Amelia asked, a sudden flush rushing to her face. She could feel Sonya looking at her.

"What she means is – have you slept with anyone?" Sonya blurted out with little tact.

Amelia felt the fear rising. Her head started to spin. Her heart was pulsating in her chest so hard that she thought it would explode. What were they implying? Was this the moment of truth? Would she have to tell them about Samuel? Had she contracted some disease from him? Her head was filled with questions. At the same time, she knew that something was wrong. All she could do was trust Sonya to keep her secret and hope that Margret would find a solution.

"Yes," Amelia's reply was a mere whisper. Sonya's mouth dropped open in disbelief. Amelia was her best friend and Sonya knew nothing of this. Sonya felt betrayed, especially since Amelia knew of all her secrets.

"You mean to tell me that you've had sex? With who?" Sonya was unrelenting. She wanted to hear the truth.

"Someone I met on the train," Amelia answered, her voice still hardly audible.

"Someone you met on the train?" Sonya asked, with sarcasm. "What, you just got into bed with some stranger who happened to be on the same train?" she asked, incredulous.

"It's not what you think Sonya," Amelia was visibly distressed, and thankful when Margret intervened.

"Wait a moment Sonya. Amelia, when was your last period girl?"

"I had it before I went to Cape Town. That was about five weeks ago."

Margret took Amelia's hands in hers. They were cold, and Amelia was trembling. The colour had drained from her face. "Amelia...I think you're pregnant."

"Oh, dear God." It was the only reaction Sonya could muster. Amelia stood still. She saw Margret's lips move as she spoke, but Amelia could not hear her. Her ears were ringing with a strange sound. All she could hear was her own voice repeating inside her head. Pregnant. Pregnant. Pregnant. All she could think about was Samuel.

It took a while for Amelia to compose herself and her thoughts. Falling pregnant with Samuel's child wasn't something she had thought possible. Now she was faced with the inevitable. If she was pregnant, she would have to face her parents and tell them the truth. It pained her to think how the news would hurt them, especially her father. Worse still, she had promised never to see Samuel again, and he would never know that she carried his child. Instinctively, Amelia knew that the symptoms she had experienced over the last few days were in fact the reality that she was with child, Samuel's child. In that instant, she realised her world was changed forever.

Amelia stood before her parents, her head lowered, resignation in her voice.

"I'm sorry, Papa. I know that you're disappointed in me, and that you are too, Ma," Amelia wanted to cry, but she fought back the tears. It was hard enough for them to accept what she had to say. She didn't want to add to their pain by being emotional about it.

"What do you know about this man, Amelia?" her mother asked, not sure what else to say.

"He's a good man, Ma. He's gentle and kind and he treated me like a lady."

"But he took advantage of you, Amelia," her mother protested.

"No, Ma. He didn't. I could have stopped him. He would never have forced himself on me. I knew what I was doing."

"Did you not stop to think of the consequences?" her mother berated.

"No! And I'm sorry. I never meant for this to happen. I'm sorry. I know how this must be hurting you both. I'm truly sorry." Amelia sat down, and let the whole truth unfold. There was no point in keeping anything from them. They were all she had, and now she would need them more than ever.

"Are you going to let him know?" her father, asked after listening without once interrupting her.

"No, Papa!" Amelia shot up off the chair. "We promised never to see each other again."

"Why if you love each other would you make such a promise?" Her father was fraught with despair.

"We are from different worlds," Amelia replied. "I didn't want us to go through life like you and Ma."

"What do you mean by that?" her mother asked.

"People always judge you and no one accepts that Papa married a coloured woman or that you married a white man. Everyone makes it seem so wrong." Amelia was trying hard to hold back the tears, but they came. Growing up, she had been shunned by coloureds and whites alike. She had never fit in, and never had a sense of belonging. Her world for nineteen years had been sheltered by her parents, her passion for art, and a handful of friends who suffered and endured the prejudices a stifled society imposed. They were considered kaffirs, undeserving of a dignified life. No one saw them as decent, law-abiding citizens. She had witnessed so often how her friends had been traumatised by white policemen who would stick a pencil through their hair and waited to see if it stayed on or fell off. On, meant frizzy and you were black. Off, meant you were white. She remembered too the night Sonya called her father in the middle of the night. One of Sonya's friend had fallen in love with a white boy, and both had been arrested because they were caught kissing on a park bench. Her friends lived in coloured townships, but she lived in a middle-class white area. Even though her parents tried to protect her from the truth, she knew. She knew that the police would track down mixed couples suspected of having relationships. Their homes were invaded, and doors smashed down before they were arrested.

"It doesn't matter what others think, Amelia," her mother said, putting her arms around her. "I married your father because I love him. Even if society says it is wrong and the law forbids it, no man has the right to pass judgement. That is for God to do."

"I know, Ma. You have both always said that love has no colour," she buried her face in her mother's chest.

"Yes, Princess, that is true." Her father took her in his arms and hugged her tenderly.

Amelia remembered the moment when Samuel had said exactly the same thing, even if he had used different words.

But they had made each other a promise. It was a promise made to keep, whatever the cost.

For the next few weeks, Amelia helped with getting the shed ready. The nausea had started to subside, and so did the irritation, which had been alleviated by some cream that Margret had recommended she use. Nothing more than that changed. Amelia was turning out painting after painting each one more beautiful and exquisite than the last. Her belly was growing with the life inside of her, and so was the bundle under her mattress, much of which paid for the costly tubes of oils, canvas, more brushes, and odds and ends she needed for the studio.

Orders for more art kept coming in, and Amelia was working very long hours, oblivious to the fact that she was eating little and sleeping even less. A visit to the hospital for a routine check-up confirmed that she needed rest, and certainly more nourishment than she was getting. At the advice of the doctor, who went to great lengths to explain that Amelia needed to take good care of herself for the baby's sake, she started to slow down. Afternoons were for napping, and her mother made sure she ate well.

It was Saturday and the first day of spring. Amelia sat outside the shed under the old oak on her favourite chair. It was an old wicker rocking chair she had picked up from a rundown second-hand shop in town. Feeling the warm rays of the sun against her skin, she found herself daydreaming. She tried hard to put Samuel out of her mind, but she couldn't. The life that he and she had created was alive and growing in her. She wondered when she would feel her unborn child move for the first time, and whether it would be a boy or a girl. Anxiety gripped at her as she wondered what the colour of the baby's skin might be. But just as quickly as the thought had come into her mind, so too did she discard it. It didn't matter. This was her child, and brown or white, it wouldn't matter. Of this she was certain.

She settled her palette and brushes on the ground and groped for the tortoiseshell clip on top of her head, releasing it so that her long curls cascaded around her face like a veil. She stood up, stretched her back and took a slow walk up to the house. Her mother was baking, and Amelia could smell the sweet and spicy aroma of vanilla cinnamon buns. They were her father's favourite, and since being pregnant she had started to favour them too. As she climbed the steps on to the veranda, her mother came out to meet her.

"There's someone on the phone for you," her mother spoke, as she wiped her hands on the apron around her waist.

Amelia entered the small entrance hall and picked up the handset.

"Hello."

"Hello Amelia, is that you?" a woman's voice asked.

"Yes, who is this?"

"It's Emma. Emma Harris. We met at the Cape fair?"

"Yes of course. How are you, Emma?" Amelia was as much pleased as she was surprised.

"In case you're wondering, I got your number from a client who has bought a fair amount of your work, Mr Phillips," Emma told her.

"Yes. I've just sent off the last painting he ordered."

"I must tell you that he raves about your work. He absolutely loves it. But that's not why I'm phoning. I need to come and see you about something I have in the pipeline. Maybe you'll be interested," Emma waited for a response.

"Sure. When do you want to meet?"

"I'll be able to get to you in about two weeks. Is that alright with you?" asked Emma.

"Sure. It will be good to see you again." Amelia gave Emma her address and they exchanged goodbyes. It was strange hearing from Emma again, but Amelia was curious to know what Emma had in mind. I'm sure I'll find out soon enough, she thought to herself and helped herself to a freshly baked cinnamon bun. The sweet mix of spices infused her senses, as the aroma wafted through the air. She was starving.

Since she last spoke to Margret, Amelia had consulted her a few times about baby things. Margret was after all a nurse, so it made sense, and Amelia was comfortable. From her conversations with Margret, Amelia knew she was into her second trimester and that her unborn child was already fully formed. She was still slender, and her belly showed only slightly, but from time to time Amelia caught herself gently feeling it as if waiting for the life inside to respond to her touch.

Emma Harris was due to arrive around lunchtime, and until then Amelia busied herself with her latest canvas. It was a painting of a woman sitting on a wicker chair under an old oak tree. It was the picture she had in her mind of herself on the first day of spring. It would be a gift for her child, a way of sharing with him or her a particular moment in her life.

It was past noon when Emma Harris arrived. She looked exactly the same as Amelia remembered her, and she greeted the older woman with a tender hug.

"It's so good to see you, child," Emma stepped back to take a look at Amelia.

"It's good to see you too."

Emma noticed instant changes in Amelia. Her hair was shinier and more lustrous than ever, and she looked radiant. She also noticed that there was a little more to Amelia hiding behind the floral smock she was wearing. Emma was a mother of three and grandmother of eight, experienced enough to recognise the 'bloom' of pregnancy, but remained silent. They walked onto the veranda where Amelia had laid a small table with two tall glasses and freshly made lemonade. They sat down, and Emma came straight to the point.

"I've been offered a great opportunity. A very prestigious gallery in Johannesburg has offered to hold an exhibition of my work," she blurted excitedly.

"That's wonderful."

"Ahh, it's a little more than that, dearie. They have invited several prominent art dealers from overseas as well. Now you know, that at this age I'm not able to turn out too many pieces and I spoke to them about including some of your work," Emma explained. "So, I'm here to find out if you're interested," she paused. "To join my exhibition that is."

Amelia was taken aback by the offer but recognised a good thing when it came her way.

"Will they agree to it?" Amelia asked, excitement mounting at the prospect of an exhibition for overseas buyers.

"Yes of course. That's why I'm here. They have agreed to let you on board, and I've ranted and raved so much about your work that they're hoping you'll say yes. I'm hoping you'll say yes," Emma was sitting on the edge of her chair.

"I don't know what to say," Amelia admitted.

"Just say yes!"

"Well then...yes, let's do it."

At that moment, Emma could no longer sit still. She almost sprung off the chair, and embraced Amelia.

"This is it child. This will catapult us to where we've dreamt of going."

Emma was too excited to be calm, and Amelia revelled in the glory of the moment. She would be exhibiting her work for international buyers. This could surely make her famous.

Just then she remembered Samuel's words, 'You'll be famous one day'. Feelings of longing for Samuel surged through every part of her being, and at that precise moment Amelia felt her baby quicken in her womb, the faint, incredible first flutter of new life. She clutched at her belly taken by surprise, and thankful that the incident had gone unnoticed by Emma.

They spent another hour going through the paperwork which Emma had brought along, and then Emma said goodbye, leaving Amelia feeling both tired and elated. Emma had brought good news indeed, but also the reality that the exhibition would take place close to the end of Amelia's pregnancy. She didn't have much stock available other than what she was painting for herself, which meant she had to produce half a dozen paintings in less than four months in time for the exhibition. Not an easy task, even for someone as young and talented as Amelia. Sipping another glass of lemonade, she sat down and placed both hands on her belly. She felt another flutter, stronger this time. She thought of Samuel, and the tears welled up. Amelia let them flow. Many were tears of joy for the miracle of life inside her, but some were of sadness and longing for a love she could never have.

Amelia's father managed to contact a truck driver who made regular trips to Johannesburg. It was someone whom he could trust, as the company he worked for used the man often to deliver goods to other provinces. Christmas came and went, and by the middle of January the truck arrived at the house to collect Amelia's paintings, all bound and carefully wrapped en route to Johannesburg. The driver was given the address of the gallery and contact number for the owner who would sign for the delivery. Amelia stood out in the street, watching as the five-ton truck disappeared down the road, and was soon obscured from view.

She could feel the pressure of the last few months. The work had taken more out of her than she wanted to admit. There had been many nights where sleep was impossible. She was overtired, and the baby often kept her awake through the night. With the truck out of view, she breathed a sigh of relief. She could slow down now and rest for a while. She needed to do that for both their sakes, as the time was getting closer and she was heavy with child.

The exhibition was due to open on the 31 January, and Emma promised to stay in touch to let her know how things were going. Between the two artists, there was a wide and varied collection of artistic talent guaranteed to astound buyers.

Amongst Amelia's collection, there were landscapes with harvests of light, colour and form, captured and preserved with evocative beauty. Scenes from the Karoo with the faint nostalgia of a landscape with simple, red-roofed, lime-washed buildings set in the distinctive olive and lichen coloured hills. There were landscapes of spring in the Overberg, when the fields of young wheat are brilliant green, and the canola flowers shine an almost fluorescent yellow against lavender shadowed mountains. And there were paintings of water, the endlessly intriguing focus of Amelia's work. Her waterscapes took the onlooker on a magical journey. Her work had the power to transport others to places one can only dream about, from the timelessness of the Karoo, to the sweet scent of a decaying riverbed or the whisper of the wind at high tide as the waves break themselves against the rocks and meander to the shore. Amelia was more than pleased, and having seen Emma's work in the past, she was convinced the exhibition would be a resounding success for both.

Alfredo and Silvia Reis were awakened by screams that pierced the silence of the night. It was past midnight when they both rushed into Amelia's room. Confronted by the pain that showed on her face, Alfredo, a man of strong will and character was rendered helpless at what he saw. Amelia's pain became a wave of spasm, tearing and wrenching at the frail body that lay soaked in sweat and blood. Rushing to her side, her mother saw that her waters had broken, and that Amelia's life was in danger. They needed to move fast.

"Get the car Alfredo…quickly!" her mother shouted. "She's haemorrhaging."

"Mama…the pain. Please…please take it away…Mama." Amelia's breathing was shallow, and she was running a high fever.

Her mother helped her sit up and covered her with the crocheted bedspread that lay at the foot of the bed.

"Hang on Amelia. Your father is getting the car. We'll be at the hospital soon," her mother tried hard to conceal the panic and fear that coursed through her veins. Amelia was in serious trouble, and Silvia fought the urge to panic. They needed to get Amelia to the hospital, nothing else mattered right now. There was no time to call an ambulance or ask questions.

Alfredo drove like a madman through the town's empty streets as if possessed by a demon. Silvia sat in the backseat and held her frail daughter in her arms as she silently prayed. They had to get Amelia there in time. God only knew how long she had been in that state.

Alfredo parked the small car outside the entrance to casualties and ran inside for help. An intern and two nurses rushed outside pushing a gurney and helped to get Amelia out from the back seat. Once inside the hospital, her parents watched as they wheeled her through the emergency doors. Their arrival had triggered a panicked frenzy. They sat huddled together in the half-lit waiting room desperate for someone to appear. But no one came. Somewhere behind the doors, the screams became less frequent until they were replaced by a cry, faint and forlorn, and then there was only silence. Alfredo felt the tears run down into the hairs of his moustache, as Silvia held his clenched fists and squeezed gently. He looked up and turned to face her, kissing the salty tears that streamed down her cheeks. It was a moment in time where no words would be necessary to express their innermost thoughts. All they could do was, wait and pray – nothing more. Their child's life lay in God's hands. Only He could decide whether she lived or died.

It was a long while before a doctor appeared in his theatre gown and flashed them a tired smile. He gestured to the door of an office. Alfredo and Silvia stood up and stared after him. The doctor sat down behind the desk and waited while they took chairs opposite him.

"How is our daughter?" Alfredo was almost too scared to ask.

"She's lost a lot of blood. The next few hours are critical." The doctor seemed hesitant to say too much.

"Will she be alright?" Silvia asked, sensing Alfredo's fear.

"It's too early to tell." The doctor was noncommittal.

"What about the baby? Is the baby fine?" Alfredo noticed that the doctor had said nothing about the infant.

"Yes. By some miracle the baby is fine. We are watching his vital signs closely. He's a very tough little boy." The doctor managed a thin smile. It was the first time that he had shown any expression. "You may see her but only for a few minutes."

A nurse showed them to the ICU where Amelia lay, connected to a drip, and several monitors. She was deadly pale and motionless. They approached the bed in silence.

Just then a nurse came into the room, holding the baby wrapped in a flannel blanket. Taking the infant in her arms, Silvia looked down at her newborn grandchild. Silvia cradled the baby close to her breast, but Alfredo bent over the body lying on the narrow bed and kissed his daughter gently on both eyes. Tiny beads of perspiration still moistened Amelia's beautiful face, her dark long hair tangled and messed, covered the flat pillow.

He stood beside the bed and raised Amelia's delicate hand to his lips. It was cold and lifeless. He allowed the tears to flow and wept in silence. The thought of losing Amelia was beyond any pain they could ever possibly imagine. God could not let that happen.

It was not until the next morning that the doctor was able to explain anything. Amelia had suffered a ruptured uterus, a condition rare in first time pregnancy, but life threatening nonetheless for both mother and child. If Amelia could get through the next few days without a relapse, the doctor was confident she would recover fully, but it was only in the privacy of his consulting room that he advised Amelia's parents of the devastating news.

"Mr and Mrs Reis..." he began, carefully choosing his words.

"Your daughter's condition is very serious. The mere fact that both she and the baby are alive is a miracle. Unfortunately, I do have some grave news..." The doctor hesitated and watched as Alfredo and Silvia shifted in their seats, their expression changing.

"But she's going to be all right, no?" asked Alfredo.

"As I said, if her condition remains stable over the next few days, I believe she will recover from this ordeal fully. Unfortunately, she will never be able to have children again." He waited and took a deep breath before finishing.

"The uterus was severely damaged, and we had no choice but to remove it." With that, the doctor leaned back in his chair. "I'm truly sorry."

The silence in the room was deafening. Silvia was the first to speak.

"Will she at least have a normal life?" her voice was fragile.

"As normal as can be expected, but it will pre-empt other physiological problems ahead of time. I suggest we discuss those at a later stage."

Alfredo sat in stunned silence. At that moment, it didn't matter to him that other problems were forthcoming. Or even that she would never bear children again. What mattered was that she was alive. They would deal with anything else later. Not now. Amelia would be well again, and then they could talk about her future.

Over the next few days, Silvia spent most of the day at Amelia's bedside. Her father would arrive straight after work. In the few days that followed, Amelia lost a lot of weight. Her beautiful face was gaunt and pale, dark circles under her eyes made them appear more sunken. Because of her condition, the baby needed supplementary feeding with bottle formula as Amelia's milk was weak and insufficient. Still even under severe pain, she marvelled at the sight of her son suckling hungrily at her breasts. It was a pain worth enduring. Ten days later, Amelia was discharged from hospital. On her way home, in the back seat of her father's car, her son cradled in her arms, the memory of that near fatal night was already a thing of the past.

The news of how well the exhibition had gone eluded both her parents, who had spent every waking hour at her bedside in the hospital ward. Now with Amelia safely at home, and life getting back to normal, they were able to share with her the good news.

The exhibition had sold out, and Amelia would probably need a bigger mattress to stash away the cash, her father teased.

As it turned out, Emma arrived at the end of February with full payment in cheques, and she let Amelia know that an art magazine wanted to do a story on her for their coffee table edition, which would be featuring prominent South African artists. Would this mean that Samuel's prophecy had come true? Was Amelia well known enough to be famous, just as

Samuel said she would be one day? Thoughts of Samuel followed her everywhere, every waking hour. And now she had Daniel to remind her of him too. He had her dark hair but his father's pale skin and green eyes.

Daniel had abounding energy, but there was also a quietness about him, which indicated from the start, a gentle disposition. He started to crawl at nine months, holding on to anything within his reach. Both grandparents doted on him, and Amelia revelled in the joy he brought into her life. Amelia spent all her free time with Daniel, showing him things, taking him places, but her favourite time with him was when she took Daniel to the bay at low tide.

"It's such a magical place," she would tell her parents. "You can hear the water rushing out, and you can hear the waves breaking in the distance but, it's calm. Daniel giggles when he sees the birds run on the sand, and I love to capture those moments."

It was this quiet appreciation of life that started to emerge in Amelia's work – paintings of anything from landscapes to people lazing on the beach, yachts in the harbour, or Daniel at play. Amelia's art had become more about her finding an inner peace and balance as much as her skill and talent kept growing.

Up until the exhibition, she had been caught up in producing paintings for several agents, but since Daniel came into her life, she had become selective, and did only specially commissioned work for the gallery in Johannesburg. Her work was now mostly available from her private gallery at the old shed studio, and people would travel to view and buy her paintings.

October 1983

Suzanne sat under the shade of the gazebo in the rose garden, enjoying a quiet reverie having tea. She was planning something special for their anniversary. Something she hoped would turn her husband around and help rekindle their relationship. For the last two years, they had sought the advice of top gynaecologists in the country. No one could determine the reasons why Suzanne was unable to conceive, and even the fertility drugs that had been induced could not bring about the one thing she longed for the most – a child.

Suzanne was a well-rounded woman, intelligent, beautiful and educated. She was an only child from a wealthy family, and as such used to being spoilt and being the centre of attention. She boasted an honours degree in music, could play the cello with perfection, and she was married to Samuel Johnston. Samuel's father had passed away from heartbreak, most believed, and that left the entire Johnston stud and estate on Samuel's shoulders. The Johnston stud established in 1948 by Samuel's father was one of the oldest in the country and had earned a fine reputation for their sheep with excellent high-quality fine wool. Over the years, the stud had expanded to optimise productivity and balance between meat and wool to ensure healthy gross margins. Samuel had also purchased several neighbouring farms, which had come his way at a price too ridiculous to turn down, but the expansion of the Johnston Stud saw the takeover of many more employees and added responsibilities, which left Samuel working long hours. He and Suzanne had married in November '81, and although at first marital bliss was most evident between them, Samuel knew his heart was lost to Amelia forever.

Quiet moments gave rise to memories of her. At times, he was tempted to go in search of her, but didn't. Because of her, he developed an interest in art and purchased many valuable pieces. His pursuit of news on up-and-coming artists became an insatiable past time. A year after he married Suzanne, he stopped torturing himself, unable to handle the torment which consumed every part of his being. He wasn't sure whether he gave up to protect Amelia, or to save himself the agony of knowing what she was up to. Thoughts of her were deeply buried in the recesses of his mind, and on occasions when he made love to his wife, sometimes several nights in succession, the one he wanted was Amelia. Haunted by guilt, he often told himself that Suzanne deserved better. Samuel loved his wife dearly, but he wasn't in love with her. To him there was a vast difference, one only he could understand. She was strikingly beautiful and womanly. Her dark long hair framed almost perfect features, and the clothes she wore accentuated her voluptuous body. She was intelligent and sharp witted, a trophy wife who possessed both beauty and brains, but there was something lacking. Something he had ever only seen in Amelia. It was something that could not be bought or fashioned in any way. Suzanne kept herself occupied playing the cello, filling her social calendar, and spending her husband's money on period furniture and collectables. Recently, she had immersed herself in a new hobby, flower arranging, in which she showed a natural ability.

Their relationship had for some time become stilted and lacking in intimacy. Partly because of their childless marriage, and partly due to Samuel's work schedule which had increased tenfold. There was distance between them, and Suzanne had become frustrated, and irritatingly demanding of Samuel's time and affection. Time, he had little left to spare, the latter he failed to demonstrate. Late nights became even longer. Suzanne ate dinner alone most evenings, and Samuel found excuses to constantly justify his absence. Unrelenting in her quest to turn things around, Suzanne was desperate to win back Samuel's love and attention. She knew he was still tempted by her naked beauty. No children meant she could keep her body beautiful and flawless, and Samuel was a passionate man. She was as sharp as she was beautiful, and she had a plan.

In their formal lounge, above the mantelpiece, was a painting of a wooded landscape. The colours of autumn leaves had always fascinated Suzanne, especially during winter when the fireplace was alight, and the red and orange ambers of the burning coals seemed to match the colours of the painting. In Samuel's office, on the wall behind the solid mahogany desk, there was another painting, a seascape so vivid that, at a glance, it sometimes appeared as if the surf spray had broken through the canvas. Although their stately home boasted an impressive collection of art, Suzanne had noticed that the workmanship of the two oil paintings was superior, and that both had been done by the same artist. This gave her an idea.

Scanning the local bookstore for flower arranging books a few days before, she stumbled across a copy of 'Quintessentially Art'. It was the latest coffee table edition of who's who in the art world, and she flipped through the glossy pages with growing interest. Suzanne read the article on Emma Harris, the 'born again artist', who, at 68 was living her dream creating a nouveau art collection. She also read about the talented Amelia Reis, who seemingly had the world's buyers at her feet. With their third wedding anniversary just a few weeks away, it would still leave Suzanne with enough time to carry out her plan. After several calls to the owner of the gallery, Suzanne was able to establish a few details about Amelia. She was young, very talented and in high demand. Her work was of an exceptional high quality, you could only contact her through the gallery, for obvious reasons, and she was an extremely private person. Understanding all this, Suzanne wanted to book her for a private sitting.

She would absorb all Ms Reis's costs. These included her transport costs to and from Graaff Reinet; accommodation at the town's best hotel; all her meals and beverages for the duration of her stay; Amelia's asking fee, and of course the gallery's incredulous booking commission. In exchange for all this, Ms Reis would produce two portraits of the client's choice which she would paint from the hotel room, and as this was a special case, all this had to be arranged under complete secrecy and with the utmost discretion.

Having understood the conditions of both parties, the gallery owner undertook to confirm final arrangements by the end of the week. Suzanne recalled the telephone conversation with the gallery early that morning as she sipped her favourite tea languidly and, smiled with girlish glee.

If this didn't win Samuel back, nothing would.

Amelia arrived in Graaff Reinet with a large easel, sheets of rolled up canvas, a leather satchel with brushes of every size, and enough oil tubes to paint the entire walls of the Cape Castle. The gallery had briefed her on the client's requirements. She was to check into the hotel and wait until the client contacted her. She had ten days to finish two life-size portraits, and the client would discuss the rest when they met. To avoid suspicion on her part, the gallery explained to Amelia the portraits were to be a surprise, hence the secrecy regarding all the arrangements.

Graaff Reinet was reminiscent of a 19th century rural town. Driving through the streets lined with magnificent Cape Dutch mansions, Amelia marvelled at the Victorian cottages with decorative 'broekie-lace' woodwork, and the splendour of a few Georgian houses. Amongst all this historic grandeur, she still caught glimpses of some flat-roofed Karoo cottages. Graaff Reinet was a town rich with period architecture, and the Drostdy Hotel built in 1806, which graced a fair part of Church Street, was undoubtedly amongst the finest. In the reception, yellow wood floors, Persian carpets, antique furniture and impressive style, awaited discerning travellers.

Alone in her room, she looked around. It was large, almost ostentatious in its setting with its own bathroom which boasted a claw-foot Victorian bath. A queen-sized four-poster brass bed with soft lace scalloped from its frame was against one wall. On one side, an antique two-door armoire in eggshell white offered ample wardrobe space. Two Cape Regency chairs with velvet cushions complimented a small round mahogany table, its dark contrasting colour softened by a vase filled with fresh cut flowers. But what captured Amelia's interest the most was an antique brass daybed near the window which faced out into the gardens. Its design matched that of the four-poster bed, and Amelia sat on it and took a deep breath.

Below, she could see the garden path lined with grapefruit trees, and wild birds feeding off suspended bird feeders hanging from several of the branches. Her client had spared no cost in making her feel comfortable, and comfortable she certainly would be as soon as she could laze in the scented water of the Victorian bath. There was always time for a little self-indulgence. Amelia unpacked, and escaped to the private luxury of the bathroom and stepped gently into the soft vapour which had filled the room as the bath filled.

The rose scented oil evaporated into the air, and Amelia closed her eyes savouring the stillness of the moment. Her senses were infused and gave way to an aroused sensuality she had not felt in a long time. Since Samuel, there had been no one. The unbridled passion that she had shared with him had lingered long after they had parted, and at times when Amelia longed to be touched, she would close her eyes and think back to their first nights on the train to Cape Town. Her hands moved softly over her breasts and then down to between her legs. She missed Samuel – all of him. With her eyes closed, she could almost feel his mouth softly on her breasts, his body pressing gently into hers and the way his hands would caress her all over, igniting the fire within her. She remembered those exquisite moments as she pleasured herself, and she knew that if not for them, it could all just be a fantasy, figments of her imagination. The experience of the bath was sublime, and Amelia felt liberated and refreshed, overcome with sensual feelings she had almost forgotten.

It was nearing noon, and still there had been no contact from her client. She decided to look around, wandering past the patio, and through to the gardens of the hotel. Apart from two couples at separate tables, the hotel was relatively quiet. Amelia meandered along the stone path, through the manicured lawn lined with neatly trimmed flowerbeds. At the far end, near a courtyard, was an imposing slave bell, reminiscent of a time when the now guest cottages were once emancipated slave quarters. On another side of the garden, an unusual structure caught her eye. Amelia approached with interest. It was a weathervane which indicated distances from Cape Town to Cairo. The thought of someday taking Daniel to see the pyramids brought a smile to her face. Someday, she thought smiling to herself. Walking back through the hotel lobby, she was met by the concierge.

"Ms Reis, your visitor has arrived, and is waiting for you in the sunroom. This way please." He escorted Amelia across the lobby to the right.

Suzanne stood up, and walked towards Amelia, offering a handshake. "Hello. You must be Ms Reis. I'm Suzanne."

"Yes. Hello." Amelia returned the handshake.

They both sat opposite each other, and Suzanne was instantly intrigued by Amelia. She was very young, and Suzanne found her to be exquisitely beautiful, delicate and refined, and alarmingly sensual. Suzanne had come to know that professionally, Amelia was an artist who had grown in stature seemingly overnight, but despite her unrelenting curiosity, Suzanne had found nothing on Amelia's private life.

"I'm sorry for keeping you waiting. I assume you've had the chance to settle in, and that the accommodations are comfortable."

"Yes, very much, thank you," Amelia answered

"Amelia…may I call you Amelia?" Suzanne asked.

"Of course."

"Amelia, I'm looking for something special and very different. I know exactly what I want in my head, but obviously I would appreciate your input as the artist." Suzanne felt a wicked tingle through her body.

"Let's discuss what you had in mind and maybe take it from there," Amelia suggested.

Suzanne took a deep breath, excitement mounting.

"I was thinking along the lines of two portraits of myself…nudes."

When Suzanne saw that Amelia didn't stir, she continued.

"I want them as a gift for my husband. We're celebrating our third wedding anniversary, and I can't think of anything he doesn't already have."

"Does your husband have an interest in art?" Amelia asked.

"Oh yes, very much so," Suzanne replied, with a slight grin.

"Then, I think your suggestion is a novel idea," Amelia replied. "I understand from the arrangements that you would like to have me paint here, in the hotel."

"Yes, under absolute secrecy of course. I presume that the room they've given you will be spacious enough?"

"Oh yes. And the setting is perfect for what you have in mind," Amelia answered, as ideas turned around in her head.

"Well, then I think that we should waste no time, and get started tomorrow morning. What time would you like me to be here?" asked Suzanne.

"Let's get going by eight if you can."

"Perfect. I will see you then. Amelia, thank you. I look forward to this. You have come very highly recommended. I know I won't be disappointed."

They parted with a handshake, and Amelia looked on, her gaze following Suzanne as she left the hotel foyer. Amelia's work had become a veritable emotional and mental fortress against invasion from the outside world, against tumultuous passions and disturbing events, those things she spent her life trying to avoid. Although not much was said, Amelia sensed a woman like Suzanne would consider such things a mystery.

Early the next morning, Amelia enjoyed another luxurious spell in the bath and a full English breakfast. She dressed in a long-flared skirt and a soft cotton shirt with buttons down the front, which accentuated her full breasts, and to which she tied in a knot at her waist. Her long tresses were tied up with a tortoiseshell hairpin, a few lose short strands framing her face. Mother-of-pearl drop earrings, a family heirloom, adorned the delicate lobes, and she wore no make-up, and no shoes. It was the way she preferred to work. Even in winter, she would pull on two pairs of thick woollen socks – but no shoes. It stopped creativity from flowing, she would often say in jest.

Amelia arranged the room in a way that would allow for the best angle and light. The drapes were pulled loosely to the sides, but not tied back, letting a soft light into the room. The daybed was turned around to face the middle of the room instead of the window, and Amelia covered it with the soft down duvet off the bed. On the floor was Amelia's bag of treasures, her tubes of paint and brushes. Suzanne arrived promptly at eight.

"Good morning," Amelia was first to speak.

"Hello again," Suzanne greeted her, as she entered the room taking in the changes already made. "You've been busy. Well, let's get started. I've brought a satin bath gown," Suzanne said, taking it out the small bag she was carrying, and holding it up for Amelia to see.

"Perfect. I love the colour. The crimson colour will blend beautifully with the brass bed." Amelia was already mixing the colour palette in her head.

"You can change in there if you like," she said, pointing to the bathroom. Amelia was rummaging through the colours when Suzanne stepped out of the bathroom.

"I want to do the first canvas with you lying on the daybed, turning around to face the window, with your back to me," she said, looking up.

"Sure," Suzanne walked over to the bed, and let the gown slip off her shoulders. She stood naked facing Amelia. "I want this to be really special, Amelia."

"It will be," Amelia said, getting up and moving towards the bed. "Let's spread the gown over here like this and prop these cushions for padding. The colour will show up your pale skin beautifully." She tossed the satin fabric lightly over the bed and arranged the cushions at one end to offer Suzanne support.

"I want you to lie on your side, and lean into the cushions," Suzanne did as Amelia suggested. "Like this?"

"Yes. Now let your arm hang over the edge and move your hand to your head as if you're resting it. Yes, that's it." Amelia moved away, and checked that the pose was right. Her hands moved over Suzanne's naked body, making small adjustments. Still not satisfied, she fetched one of her hairpins from the bathroom, and taking Suzanne's hair in her hands tied it up, leaving soft wispy curls cascading down her back.

"It looks better with a full view of your back, a more sensual line," Amelia explained.

"Are you comfortable enough?" Amelia asked, getting ready.

"As comfortable as I'm going to be, I guess," Suzanne replied.

"It will be a while but let me know if you need a break."

Suzanne nodded in agreement and took a deep breath. She was recalling the sensation of Amelia's touch on her bare skin and felt an inexpressible tingle surge through her. She gazed out the window, through the lace drapes and tried to remember to keep still. Amelia sat at the easel and found herself admiring Suzanne's body. She was slender, but well accentuated with voluptuous curves. Her skin was a creamy white, flawless and with good muscle tone. It was the first time that Amelia was painting a nude from real life, and the experience left her with an unexpected twinge of excitement. It was also the first time that she found herself in such proximity to a naked woman. Amelia started on the canvas. Something in the power and urgency of her brush strokes suggested a restlessness she couldn't quite fathom.

Throughout the day, Amelia kept her mind focused on her work. At night, when all was still, and she lay awake, sleep eluded her, and she tried to shut out visions of Suzanne. Amelia thought about Suzanne's curvaceous hips and full breasts. How the small of her back compressed subtly to form a tiny dimple above each buttock. How her slender neck created an elegant line to a near perfect body. Amelia unwillingly found herself aroused by Suzanne's nudity, but also by a burning desire to explore her own sexuality.

Toiling through the nights that brought no comfort to the aching she felt inside, Amelia put the finishing touches on the painting ahead of schedule.

She had become anxious, unsure of how to deal with what she was feeling, and she suggested to Suzanne that they start with the second painting without delay. Confused by mixed emotions, Amelia longed for the safety of her own home, and for Daniel. When Suzanne arrived to discuss the second portrait, Amelia felt tension building in her body.

"Why don't we send for room service? I could do with something refreshing to drink," Suzanne suggested.

"I think I prefer just stretching my legs a little, if that's alright with you." Amelia didn't trust herself. Not the way she was feeling.

"Sure. We can have some tea in the garden, and maybe discuss what you have in mind for the next painting." Suzanne smiled.

With a cool wind blowing outside, they decided to chat in the sunroom instead.

"Tell me a little about what you do, Suzanne," Amelia spoke first.

"You mean work wise?" asked Suzanne.

"I was thinking more along personal interests," Amelia could feel a warm glow on her face. Had she asked the question correctly, she wondered.

"Well, I play the cello, and most recently started a new hobby, flower arranging. I know it sounds simple, but dabbling around with flowers is actually very therapeutic," she continued.

"Anything involving nature is inspiring. I think it's wonderful. And we could use that for your next painting," Amelia said, her mind already searching for ideas.

"We will need a little extra something."

Suzanne was looking at her quizzically. "Like what?" she asked.

"We need a piece of jewellery. Something in silver would be perfect," Amelia replied.

"I have an antique bracelet that's set in silver."

"Bring it with you tomorrow. And another thing, could you arrange for the hotel to send up a fresh arrangement of mixed flowers?" Amelia asked.

"Of course. I'll make sure you have whatever you need." Suzanne took another sip of her tea, and sitting back in the cane armchair, eyed Amelia with renewed interest.

"So, tell me a little about you. I read about your rise to fame, but what about the private Amelia?" Suzanne ventured, but tread lightly.

"Not much to tell really." Amelia was hesitant to share anything about her private life.

"Do you have a special someone in your life, maybe?" Suzanne tried another angle.

"Oh yes," Amelia answered fondly, as she thought of Daniel.

"Any big plans with this special someone?"

"Not for a long while," Amelia replied.

"Have you ever been in love, Amelia?" asked Suzanne.

"Why do you ask?"

"I'm curious. Passion shows so vividly in your work. Art, like love, is rarely appreciated until there is a danger of losing it." Suzanne was prying, Amelia knew that.

"Yes. Once, but it was never meant to be." Suzanne's curiosity mounted, but she sensed Amelia's reluctance to share any details of her life and backed off.

"I'm sorry."

It was time to go. They confirmed the arrangements for the next day, and parted. Amelia felt lightheaded and found herself suddenly engulfed by a strong sense of loss. Samuel. His name echoed in her mind. Back in the safety of her room, she broke down. Leaning against the solid door for support, Amelia cried uncontrollably, not just for herself, but for the love she gave up. She crawled into bed, and lay shivering, curled tightly in a ball, smothered in the down comforter. She felt ill, and lonely and afraid. Her body hurt from the wrenching sobs. Her pain was insurmountable, her loss too great to endure. Samuel. Samuel. Stunned by the abruptness of her loss and the puzzling vacuum that followed, Amelia fell into a dreamless sleep.

The night seemed somewhat longer which she was thankful for, and Amelia welcomed the new day, feeling more rested. Perhaps all she needed was a good cry. Other than a melancholy feeling, she showed no visible signs of the night before. Suzanne arrived promptly as before.

Amelia wanted to create a very different mood for the second painting, something coy yet evocative, and set up the room in the exact way she wanted to capture it.

The oak table was moved against the blank wall. One of the chairs stood to the side of the table, and the arrangement of flowers in the antique vase, which had been delivered earlier were in full bloom, alive with vibrant colour and subtle fragrance. Suzanne walked towards the chair, wearing only a champagne coloured satin gown and an antique bracelet on her right wrist.

"I would like you to sit, legs crossed but relaxed, and leaning slightly more onto your right hip towards the table," Amelia said, moving away just a little.

"Like this?" Suzanne checked.

"Yes. Now let your left arm fall loosely to the side and bring your right hand to rest on the vase. Close your eyes and tilt your chin slightly forward. That's it. Perfect." Amelia moved Suzanne's hair over her left shoulder, leaving it to fall naturally just above her full breast. She was ready to start.

Sitting at her easel, Amelia realised that it took more than professionalism to contain her feelings, much more. It required that she quench the burning desire that rushed through her body. In her mind, images of Samuel as he made love to her coursed through her veins like an electric current. She was consumed with a desire to touch and be touched, and every part of her being was crying out for release. She could only hope that Suzanne wouldn't notice.

Three days later, Amelia finished the second portrait. Up until then, Suzanne hadn't seen the finished work, and when she arrived at Amelia's door, her excitement was almost tangible. Confronted by her own nakedness, Suzanne was in awe. Amelia had captured the true essence of her femininity, and Suzanne took some time to admire the fine detail.

"These are exquisite, Amelia," She commented, as she moved to embrace Amelia.

"I'm glad you're pleased," Amelia replied, returning the embrace. Without warning, Suzanne touched her lips to Amelia's. Instead of withdrawing, Amelia found herself responding, as a warm sensation gushed through her whole body.

"You are talented and stunningly beautiful, Amelia, and you excite me." Suzanne ran her hands down Amelia's back. Amelia found herself doing the same.

"Touch me Amelia," Suzanne whispered, almost pleadingly. Without hesitating, Amelia slipped her hands underneath Suzanne's thin silk blouse. The softness of the fabric only served to arouse her even more and Suzanne breathed deeply as Amelia undid the small pearl buttons, one by one, letting the blouse fall to the floor. Underneath, Suzanne's erect nipples pressed hard into the thin lace petticoat. Taking Amelia by the hand, Suzanne moved towards the bed and sat down. Amelia sat beside her and slipped the silky petticoat off Suzanne's slender shoulders and down to her waist, before gently pushing her back onto the bedcovers. Suzanne took shallow breaths and groaned with pleasure as Amelia's sensuous lips kissed her full breasts, sending her into the throes of unabated ecstasy. Amelia breathed in Suzanne's sweet female scent, mingled with the soft perfume she was wearing. Suzanne treasured the silken tickle of Amelia's hair against her face, and Amelia remembered how it had been with Samuel the first time when he had loved her, inside her, making her his. Both women became lost in a reverie of uninhibited desire unlike anything Suzanne had ever experienced. After Suzanne left and night came, Amelia could feel the months and years of pent up desire and longing for the passion she had experienced so briefly in her life.

Suzanne arrived at the Drosty Hotel to say goodbye. Amelia would be on her way home, and Suzanne was no longer sure of herself anymore, wasn't sure of anything at all, except how much she needed Amelia, and longed for the shelter of her arms. She'd had a sleepless night, unable to shake off thoughts of their encounter. She had made love to Samuel, but something was amiss. It was as though Amelia had unlocked in her some secret room to which she wanted to go to willingly and unbidden. Suzanne was vulnerable, and almost driving herself crazy as she tried to revive her marriage and Samuel's interest in her. Somehow, Amelia unknowingly gave her a new sense of purpose, made her feel womanly and erotically sensual.

"I'm sad to see you go," Suzanne uttered in a soft voice, as she took Amelia's hand, leading her to the large bed. They laid side by side. Suzanne turned, and touched her lips to Amelia's cheek. She found herself wanting and waiting for Amelia's delicate and sensual touch. Amelia rolled toward her and put her arm around her. And at her touch, Suzanne couldn't help but cry. "I need you, Amelia."

Amelia saw in Suzanne's eyes, the frailty of her heart, the longing for something lost. She understood only too well the intensity of such deep-rooted pain, the longing, and the hope of finding what was lost. There was no plan. There was only the slow, inexorable conjunction of two wounded souls.

Suzanne turned towards her and put her arm around Amelia's waist and felt the warmth of her body, the shapes and angles of her, the press of Amelia's body against her breasts. Desire snapped like a tight line through Suzanne's core as she stroked Amelia's hair. Suzanne allowed herself to be led again to a place she had never been to before. It was a place of reckless abandon, and Suzanne understood that her life would never be the same. For Amelia, their brief intimate encounters served to remind her of the exquisiteness of the way Samuel had loved her. For Suzanne, it was a journey into the hidden depths of fantasy – as she discovered just how far she would go in search of seduction, surrender, and pleasure beyond imagining. Something she had never experienced before with anyone, before Amelia.

Sitting in the opulent surroundings of their formal lounge sipping on Napoleon Brandy, Suzanne felt a girlish excitement as she anticipated Samuel's reaction to her anniversary gift. She sat on the arm of the double sofa and ran her fingers through his hair before kissing him.

"Thank you for dinner, Suzanne. It was superb," he said, taking her hand to his lips and planting a gentle kiss.

"I have another little surprise for you, darling," she said, taking his hand, and leading him into the library. Suzanne made her way towards the tall easels in the corner and unveiled the two paintings, dropping the white sheets to the floor. "These are my gift to you, my love."

"Suzanne!" he managed, catching his breath. "These are beautiful. I don't know what to say."

"Say you love me, and that I'm beautiful. And that you tolerate me because you love me," she said, putting her arms around his neck.

"You are a beautiful woman Suzanne. And you know I love you." Samuel wanted so much to believe his own words, but he couldn't. He loved his wife, but he wasn't in love with her. He had never been in love with her. It hurt him to know that. But it hurt him more to know that he had let the love of his life slip through his fingers. He could have stopped Amelia. He could have broken his promise to her and tried to find her. For four years, he had lived with her memory, and it kept eating away at him like a growing, cancerous wound. He understood the demise of his father. The old man had died of a broken heart. Without the woman who had shared forty years of his life, there was nothing left to live for. Samuel had begun to understand this. Without Amelia he would continue to merely exist.

Samuel admired the paintings from a distance, not close enough to notice the artist's name.

"I had them done by one of the country's finest artists," Suzanne mentioned, when Samuel became quiet.

"So, this is where you kept running off to." Samuel tried to conceal his anguish. To disguise the pain that tore into him like the cut of a switchblade.

"It was meant to be a surprise, so I couldn't well let you into my little secret, could I?" The thought sent a mischievous little smile to her lips.

"They're exceptional." A thin smile touched his lips.

"So, who is this talented artist? Will I have to kill him?" Samuel managed light-heartedly.

"She. A young artist named Amelia Reis. I doubt she's older than 25," Suzanne said casually.

Twenty-three, Samuel heard himself saying. Hoping the words had not escaped his lips. At the mention of her name, Samuel froze. Struggling to move, Samuel turned and walked slowly towards the paintings, too afraid of what he would see. He lifted his right hand to the canvas and traced her name with his fingers. Amelia Reis. He stood dead still, unable to move away, as if the sight of her name alone was a giant magnet, drawing him toward her.

"Samuel? Are you alright?" Suzanne asked, concerned. "Darling you've gone awfully pale. Is something wrong?"

"I think I'm just tired. I need to get an early start. That group of Australians are due day after tomorrow. There's still a lot of paperwork to sort out before we meet." It was the only reasonable excuse Samuel could come up with. The shock of knowing that Amelia had been so near left him in a catatonic state. Worse, still, was finding out she and Suzanne had been in such proximity of each other.

"Thanks again for dinner, and your gift." Samuel kissed her on the cheek, and turned away, retreating to his study. He sat at the large mahogany desk and turned around to stare at the painting behind him. At the time he had bought the painting from Amelia, she was still unknown, and had signed off her work with just two capital letters, AR. Now four years later, Amelia was famous, just as he had predicted she would be, and she used her full name. He doubted Suzanne was aware that AR and Amelia Reis were one and the same person. The irony bemused Samuel, and he let out an almost inaudible chuckle that became wrenching sobs from somewhere deep in his soul.

The seasons passed, marked by the changing colours of the countryside. Amelia stood in the middle of the open field on their property, trying to teach Daniel how to fly a kite. A strong autumn wind was blowing, and no sooner did she manage to get the kite up in the air than it would come plummeting down, nose first into the ground. Daniel found the whole experience amusing and let out shrieks of laughter at Amelia's comical antics. It was an endearing moment for a humble mother who had hardly been prepared for the greatest job on earth. Putting the kite down, Amelia took Daniel's hand and ran with him through the heaps of fallen leaves. They rolled on the ground, and Daniel chuckled heartily as Amelia allowed him to cover her with handfuls of dry leaves. Amelia loved the colours of autumn, which always brought a warm gentle glow to her world. Winter was the hardest season for her to bear. Not because of the cold, but because it gave rise to so many memories of long ago.

Something in Amelia had changed since her return from Graaff Reinet. She had grown as a person and as a woman, and she had come to know herself a little more differently. She knew then that pride as well as fear had stood between her and Samuel. She alone had passed judgement on what they had. It was fear that had stood in the way of their love, not racial prejudice. The ban imposed on mixed marriages and sexual relations between black and white was becoming something of the past by the time her and Samuel had met. Yet, the irrevocable past continued to haunt her future. She also knew that Samuel would have followed her to the end of the world, if only she had allowed him to. And although fate drove them apart, they were joined forever – by Daniel.

Amelia built a place for herself and Daniel on her parent's small property. Having them close was a constant source of comfort for her, especially when she travelled to different places in search of fresh ideas and inspiration. During those times away from home, she was at ease knowing Daniel was well taken care of. Her mother had since been home to take care of Daniel, whilst Amelia worked in the studio. But Daniel, who was almost four and growing up fast, had plenty of quality time with his mother. The old studio had been extended to expand Amelia's private gallery, and a section was closed off as a back room where Amelia gave art lessons to disadvantaged neighbourhood children.

At the Johnston Stud, life since finding out about Amelia, had become different for Samuel and Suzanne. Weeks had elapsed, and work kept Samuel busy, but he was overly distracted by recurring thoughts of Amelia. Life became almost unbearable. He sensed a change in Suzanne, something he couldn't put his finger on, but her lovemaking had become more intense, with an urgency that hadn't been there before, and at times he found himself giving in to her wanton. He wanted to succumb to Suzanne and her increasing needs, hoping to lose himself and dispel feelings of despair, but instead he found himself torn between the loyalty to his wife, and his undying love for Amelia. He saw her in every corner of his house. He imagined her in every waking moment, and he felt her in his arms every time he shared an intimate moment with Suzanne. There were days he thought he would go out of his mind, and he knew, the day of reckoning was near. It was time to confront Suzanne. Avoiding the truth would only prolong the intense suffering he endured, knowing he should be with Amelia, that he should go in search of her.

After dinner, they sat in the lounge. The burning logs in the fireplace cast gentle shadows around the room. Samuel had felt melancholy all day, and whilst it was warm around the fire, he felt as cold as the winter air outside.

"Suzanne, there is something important I need to discuss with you." There was no easy way out, and Samuel knew that.

"Why so serious?" Suzanne picked up on his uneasiness, as he got up from the armchair.

"I know that for some time now, I haven't been much of a husband. At least, not the kind of husband you were hoping for."

"Yes, but you've been busy, and you have the trip to Australia coming up soon, I understand that," Suzanne replied.

"It's not just the work Suzanne. Work has been an excuse to avoid the truth." Samuel searched for words.

"Avoid what truth?" Suzanne asked, slowly sitting upright. Samuel wished he could have found a way to soften the blow.

"Suzanne, you are a good woman, and a beautiful one at that and you deserve more." Samuel stood before her, hands in his pockets, but his gaze was directed at the painting above the fireplace.

"Samuel, what is it? What are you trying to say?" Suzanne felt panic in her voice as she spoke.

"I don't believe I'm the man for you."

"Isn't that for me to decide?" She felt her cheeks prickle.

Samuel wanted to say what he must, without causing her too much pain. But how could it not be painful for her when it was so for him?

"I'm in love with someone else, Suzanne. And I will always love her." Samuel could hardly believe his words. He felt empty but free. "I'm sorry, Suzanne. I've never wanted to hurt you." He was filled with despair and relief all at the same time.

"You're in love with someone else? Have you ever loved me, Samuel?"

"Yes, but it's not enough. It's not the love you deserve, and I can't go on living the lie. I'm sorry."

"How long have you been in love with this woman?" Suzanne tried hard to stay composed.

"Long before you and I even met."

"I don't understand," Suzanne admitted.

Samuel felt a strange sense of calm come over him as he sat down again on the armchair facing Suzanne.

"Who is she anyway? Do I know her?" Suzanne was now more curious to know, and she felt anger welling up.

"It's Amelia." The sound of her name on his lips filled him with courage.

"Amelia?" she blurted out, incredulous. "Amelia Reis, the artist?" Suzanne was dumbstruck.

There was no turning back now, and Suzanne had the right to know the truth. Samuel could only hope that the truth would set him free. His love for Amelia was something he could no longer hide. Not from Suzanne or himself. It was time to stop running away from the truth. It was the same truth that had kept him a prisoner of his own mind for years. Ever since the day they parted, that winter, at Grand Central Station. Amelia had taken his heart with her. It would never be his to give again.

"As hard as it may be for you to understand Suzanne, she was my first love. And I was hers." He almost choked on his words.

"So, what happened?" Suzanne experienced mixed feelings of betrayal and empathy for him. She too had experienced something rare with Amelia, but it wasn't something she could ever tell. Not to him, or anyone, and in a way, she almost understood his desperation.

"We parted, promising never to seek the other one out. In her mind, ours was a love that would only bring us pain."

"Did she ever tell you why she felt that way?" Suzanne wanted to understand but was puzzled.

"She's coloured. Born from a white father and coloured mother." Saying those words tore at him like a dagger.

Shocked, Suzanne remembered her conversation with Amelia and what she had said, 'it was never meant to be'.

Samuel brought his hands to his face and cried. They were tears he could no longer hold back. He had let Amelia slip away. For four years, he had tried to forget her. Now, faced with knowing that she had been so close, became too much.

Suzanne sat beside him, feeling his pain, his loss. She cradled his face, holding him so their gazes locked, so she could look into his eyes, and feel what he felt for Amelia.

"The first time I saw her, I loved her. Just like that. The way the stars shine, just because they do. The way the wind blows, just because it must. I love her, and nothing will ever change that. Not time, not even death," his voice was filled with emotion.

"If you stay, you'll come to resent me, and I love you too much for that," Suzanne's voice was soft, gentle, and the compassion showed in her eyes, brimming with tears.

"I'm so sorry, Suzanne. I never ever meant to hurt you."

"I believe you. Go to her. It's where you belong. Honour what you feel, Samuel. And don't let anything stand in your way." Suzanne kissed him tenderly. She stood up, and looked down at Samuel, fragile, and ever so vulnerable. She stroked the top of his head gently, then turned away knowing that he was lost to her forever.

A bad bout of flu, that had developed into bronchitis, left Amelia weak and frail for several days. She was in the studio's back room taking stock on supplies, when the phone rang in the gallery. "Hello." It was Marius Stein, the gallery owner.

"I am yes, much better, thank you," Amelia replied.

"Did he mention anything specific?" Amelia asked, as he briefed her over the phone.

"I see. Yes, I should be able to make the deadline. Did he say when he'll pick it up?" asked Amelia.

"I'll make sure it's ready by then. And, thank you," Amelia replaced the receiver.

Marius Stein had called to order a painting for a new client. It had to be a seascape that was to include any form of human life, which he would leave up to her to choose. Price wasn't an issue as she had been highly recommended to him. The client was at present abroad and would be returning mid-June at which time he was planning to collect the painting himself.

Painting a seascape in the middle of winter after she'd just spent two weeks huddled up in bed with bronchitis was a ludicrous idea. Her parents advised her against it, but Amelia had already made up her mind.

For some unexplainable reason, Amelia felt inspired to create something special. She decided to travel to the coast and take Daniel with her. With promises to call home each day, and the assurance that she would return home immediately if she started to feel unwell, Amelia left home joined by Daniel, who was looking forward to going to the beach. They found accommodation at a bed and breakfast off the beaten track. It was cosy and quaint, and within walking distance from a secluded stretch of beach. She had the sea view and her muse. The rest would be born out of her imagination.

As the painting started to unfold, Amelia found a new wave of inspiration flow through her. For most of the week, she found herself in a strange silent reverie, which lingered well into the night as she cradled Daniel in her arms under the bed covers.

The painting was that of a young child, hair blowing in the breeze, picking seashells along the shore. From the moment Amelia started painting, she sensed a new kind of excitement. It was an experience that lifted her to new heights of certainty, and self-belief about what it meant to be an artist. Seeing Daniel come alive on the canvas changed the way she needed to look at life. For the first time, Amelia sensed an intelligence in her son, a wordless, natural intelligence that had escaped her before. She sat watching him with a rapturous smile on her face, listening to his little voice trailing off in the breeze. Her enlightenment was clouded by a sense of fragility she could not explain.

As they travelled home a few days later, she gazed at the landscape with its patchwork of different hues and saw all its beauty in a different way from before. She was growing as an artist, and maturing as a mother, but she had stopped living. Amelia was well aware that she had survived the last four years on memories to help her through each passing day, and it was time to let Samuel go.

The yearning for him and the longing for his love clouded so many moments in her life, and it kept her heart tightly shut. She needed to open her heart to be loved again.

Picking Seashells was by far Amelia's most exquisite work. It was also the first work that she named, even though she was unsure of the reasons why. Perhaps, it was because Daniel was a part of it. Or, maybe because, by capturing Daniel in such a way brought her comfort, knowing that in him Samuel and the love they shared would never be forgotten. She was twenty-four years old, successful, and a world-renowned artist. It was time to let go the ghosts of the past.

Amelia accepted Sonya's invitation to a party with some friends, which seemed a good way to start moving forward. Besides, it had been some time since she'd been out, and her friend joked about Amelia becoming an old maid. Sonya could be very persuasive.

The music was loud, and Amelia found herself surrounded by people she'd never met. In the past, she would have enjoyed the dancing and joined in the chatter, but so much about her had changed. Standing alone in a corner deep in thought, she didn't notice as a young man approached.

"Would you like to dance?" he asked. Amelia was staring at him, unable to hear over the loud music.

"I said...would you like to dance?" he asked, again.

"Sorry. No. Thanks." She felt as if she were in a tiny room that was getting smaller with each breath she took.

"Could I get you a drink then?" he persisted.

Amelia stared at him, and then looked around. All at once, a wave of dizziness filled her head, and her ears where ringing with the sound of a thousand cymbals. She needed to get out. She needed to breathe. Something inside was choking her. Her heart raced, and her palms became clammy, and Amelia felt the ground fall away from under her.

When she came around, Amelia lay in the backseat of Sonya's car. She was running a high temperature and her breathing had become shallow. She tried to assure her best friend that she'd be all right, but Sonya wasn't convinced. Back home, her father called the local doctor who fortunately still did house calls. Under the doctor's orders, Amelia was confined to bed rest. Her chest was tight, and breathing became difficult, and the coughing had started again. She had not recovered completely from the bronchitis, and the cold and dampness at the coast had triggered off the inflammation again. This time she was wise to follow the advice given by the doctor and her parents, and Daniel made sure she followed orders. He sat at the foot of Amelia's bed, as he assembled his large pieces of Lego.

The incident at the party convinced Amelia she wasn't ready to open her heart to anyone else. Not now, and not in a long time to come. A part of her felt that she would never be ready. The day she gave herself to Samuel was the day she had given away her heart and soul. Daniel was a living reminder of that, and there was no one she loved more deeply than her son, but she was also filled with an emptiness that at times bordered on inexpressible despair. There were often times when the longing to be with Samuel would tempt her to go in search of him, but something always held her back. It was no longer pride that stopped her, but the fear of finding him, and not knowing what he would do. It was the fear of not knowing whether he loved her still. It was the fear of finding him in love with someone else and lost to her forever. Feelings of desperation and hopelessness made it impossible for her to reason, but worse still, was the anguish of regret.

A call from Marius Stein alerted Amelia of her client's intention to collect the painting he'd ordered. He was due to arrive the following morning, although Marius Stein was unable to confirm the time. The painting was ready, and Amelia marvelled at the way Picking Seashells spoke to her. It was as if Daniel alone had breathed life into the canvas. She closed her eyes and replayed the images of those few days in her mind. The way Daniel's little body bent down to pick shells, and the excitement in his voice as he ran to show her another one of his finds.

Amelia's fee had more than trebled in four years. Now, she was a sought-after artist whose reputation preceded her. Her clients were some of the country's most influential people, and her work was exported and exhibited abroad. Despite all the fortune and glory, Amelia was still the same person she had always been. With Daniel and the neighbourhood children, she had found her purpose. Love, she often thought, would come by again perhaps one day. On a day when she no longer surrendered herself to the memory of Samuel. She was still lost in thought when she heard footsteps. Thinking it was Daniel, she turned around to greet him, a radiant smile, lighting up her face.

"Hello, Amelia," Samuel stood in the doorway, and Amelia had to steady her body against the wall to stop herself from falling.

"Samuel." She could hardly hear her own voice. It seemed so very far away.

"What are you doing here?" she asked, too afraid to move away from the wall in case she stumbled.

"I've come to fetch my painting," he answered.

"Your painting?" she gasped, as the colour drained from her face. "Yes, didn't the gallery call you?"

"Yes, but they di..." Amelia was dizzy and found it difficult to breathe as her heart thumped in her chest.

"Are you all right?" he asked, concerned.

"Yes. Of...of course."

"Is this the one?" He pointed towards the easel.

Amelia nodded. The words stuck in her throat. Samuel was the client, and Samuel was standing right before her. Four years gone, and he was exactly as she remembered him on the day they parted on the station platform in Cape Town. If not for Daniel, who came running into the gallery at that moment, Amelia would have thought that she was in the middle of a dream, or a terrible joke. This couldn't be so. This moment could not be real. It was not happening, and yet as Daniel ran into her arms, Amelia knew that it was no dream.

Samuel looked down at Daniel as he approached the painting, then turned to face Amelia.

"This is beautiful, Amelia." She saw the gleam in his green eyes.

"And who is this?" he asked, looking at Daniel.

"This is Daniel, my son," Amelia replied, her voice shaky, her admission taking Samuel by surprise.

"He's the child in the painting, right?" He looked at Daniel again, and then at the painting.

"Yes."

"So, you're married, then?" Samuel didn't want to pry, but he had to know.

"No." Amelia wanted to tell him the truth. She wanted to let Samuel know that Daniel was their son, every part of her was crying out. This was the moment she had imagined so many times before, ever since the day she found out she was carrying his child. They had made each other a promise, and for four years she had kept that promise. Was Samuel just another client, or did he break his promise to come looking for her? She was afraid to ask, too afraid of what she might hear. Feeling her heart rate return to normal, she bent down to speak to Daniel.

"Daniel, go up to Nana, my darling. Mama will be there in a little while." And she sent him off with a kiss on his head.

"He's beautiful, Amelia, and he's very lucky to have you as his mother." Samuel was overcome with emotion. He wanted nothing more than to take her in his arms and hold her. There was so much he wanted to say. The silence between them became uncomfortable.

"The gallery didn't give me any names. I didn't know who..." Amelia tried to explain.

"I asked them not to. I was afraid that if you knew you wouldn't have taken on the work." Samuel moved around, looking at the paintings hanging on the walls. He liked the ambiance, the lack of pretence, and the way the sunlight angled through the slats of the wooden shutters.

"How did you know where to find me?" Amelia wanted to know.

Samuel gave a thin smile. "It was through my wife, actually."

"Your wife?" Amelia's heart sank. So, Samuel had moved on. But then again, why shouldn't he have? It was she who had driven him away. He had stayed away, just as she had made him promise he would. What did she expect?

"How so?" Amelia swallowed hard.

"You did some work for her," he said, turning to face her.

"I did?" Amelia was more puzzled than ever.

"Yes, two paintings, in fact, both quite exquisite." Samuel could see the confusion in her face. "They were a gift, for our anniversary to be precise."

Her heart was racing again. Her mouth went suddenly dry and she found it hard to swallow.

"Suzanne Johnston is your wife?" Her chest felt tighter, and her head was spinning out of control.

"Was, we agreed to go our separate ways." Samuel watched her.

"I'm sorry." Amelia wasn't sure whether she felt compassion or relief.

"Don't be. It wouldn't have worked out for us. I told her the truth."

"The truth?" Amelia ventured, trying to regain composure.

"That I could only love one woman. You, Amelia."

There. He had finally said it. All this time wasted. All the time he was standing there in front of her, he could have told her from the start.

Overwhelmed by his candour, Amelia didn't want to think about what Suzanne might have told him. She hoped he was oblivious of their intimate encounters.

"I don't know what to say Samuel. This is so unexpected."

"You don't have to say anything at all. We parted as friends. Besides, I think Suzanne had plans of her own."

Amelia felt the colour rise in her cheeks. Had Suzanne told him? Samuel knew beyond all doubt that there was no turning back for him. He loved Amelia, and he had come for her. But was she free?

"What about you?" Samuel could feel his heart pounding all the way up his throat.

Samuel felt a sinking feeling. Amelia avoided his questioning look.

"Do you love him?" Samuel wanted to look in her eyes.

"Forever," Amelia whispered. "As much as I love our son."

Samuel stepped away from her, confusion spinning in his head. "What are you saying?"

"That you have a son. Daniel is your son. There has never been anyone other than you." Amelia tried hard to hold back the tears welling up behind her eyes. Samuel took her in his arms, and held her tight against him, a tidal wave of emotion sweeping over them both. They had been away from each other, but never apart. Amelia leaned her head against his shoulder in response. Her dark hair shone with the soft radiance of the morning light, and her womanly beauty struck him speechless. His chest warmed at the emotional connection. His arms embraced the fulfilment of a dream and a reason to be alive.

"You have no idea how I have waited for this moment," Samuel managed between sobs. But she knew only too well.

He lifted her hands to his lips and kissed the tips of her fingers. "We have a lot to talk about."

She nodded, and said, "Yes," but her voice caught in her throat.

"Don't cry," he said, leaning in to kiss her cheek. "I love you, Amelia. Do you believe that?"

"Yes," she whispered faintly, no louder than a breath.

In that instant, Samuel realised that love climbs into your heart through your eyes and hides there until you're ready for it. He looked into her eyes and saw so much love there that it was almost impossible to breathe.

"I remember so clearly the day you walked into my life," he whispered, holding her close. "Life has meant nothing to me without you in it."

They stepped out of the gallery with arms around each other. The cold air stung their tear streaked faces. They had met in winter, on a day not too different from this. Amelia looked up to the sky with its kaleidoscope of grey hues and said a silent prayer as Samuel held her closer.

"I love you Amelia, and I never want to lose you again."

She had come full circle. In the middle of an African winter, Amelia had taken the journey that changed her life in the most unimaginable ways. But at that very moment, winter's cold breath had found a way to warm her heart forever. She savoured the comfort of Samuel's arm around her shoulders, the closeness of his cheek against her head, and the gift of his love that would warm her world forever.